Prelude
to a
Seduction

Prelude
to a
Seduction

LOTCHIE BURTON

CRIMSON
ROMANCE
F+W Media, Inc.

Crimson Romance
an imprint of F+W Media, Inc.
10151 Carver Road, Suite 200
Blue Ash, Ohio 45242
www.crimsonromance.com

ISBN 10: 1-4405-7348-4
ISBN 13: 978-1-4405-7348-4
eISBN 10: 1-4405-4457-3
eISBN 13: 978-1-4405-4457-6

Printed in the United States of America.

10 9 8 7 6 5 4 3 2 1

This is a work of fiction. Names, characters, corporations, institutions, organizations, events, or locales in this novel are either the product of the author's imagination or, if real, used fictitiously. The resemblance of any character to actual persons (living or dead) is entirely coincidental.

Many of the designations used by manufacturers and sellers to distinguish their product are claimed as trademarks. Where those designations appear in this book and F+W Media was aware of a trademark claim, the designations have been printed with initial capital letters.

Cover image © 123rf.com.

This book is available at quantity discounts for bulk purchases.
For information, please call 1-800-289-0963.

Dedication

To Susan Atlas. Thank you for seeing my potential years before I ever did.

To Cathy Ray, Belinda Bourecksky, Denise Jackson, Valencia Abrams, and Janine Blossom. Thank you all for being my confidante, my sounding board, and my friend. I would not have made it this far without your encouragement, your input, and your availability.

Prologue

"What are you doing?"

"I'm undressing you," he murmurs as his fingers deftly unfasten the buttons of her blouse and unzip her skirt. His mouth teases and nibbles at her neck and shoulder.

"Silly man, of course you're undressing me." She giggles. "Maybe my question should have been *why?*"

"Because," he whispers in her ear and lets his lips journey down her cheek to trail kisses across her chin and lips. "I love to touch your skin, and I can't touch you with all these clothes on."

Her smile is warm and sexy; her breath is hot and sweet. "I know, but if you keep this up, I'll never get out of here on time."

"That's the plan," he says, showing off perfect, beautiful white teeth in a wide, wolfish grin.

"I can't be late, not again!" She shrieks with laughter when he leans forward and licks that elusive sensitive spot just behind her ear.

"I'll bet no one will even notice. Come on, babe, let me send you off with a smile on your face," he cajoles. "Or at least let me send you off with a smile on *my* face." He grins and wiggles his eyebrows up and down. She shakes her head. He knows she'll eventually give up and give in to his persuasive mouth and convincing hands. Ignoring her feeble attempts at protest, he continues to methodically strip her clothing away piece by piece until she stands completely naked and exposed to his appraising gaze. He lays her down upon the bed and blankets her with his body, burying his face between her soft, succulent breasts.

"Mmm," he sighs in muffled contentment. "You feel so soft. I could lie here forever."

"We don't have forever," she purrs seductively, "and I can't wait that long. You've got me naked; you need to do something about it right now."

"I'm more than happy to oblige, my lady," he responds, his voice low and husky with need. "Your demand is my wish." He brushes and strokes her body with nimble fingers and knowledgeable hands, familiar with every curve, every dip, and every hollow. He knows her body in intimate detail, and he knows what it takes to make her hum, purr, and sing for him.

"I love the way you smell. You smell like ice cream," he murmurs and slowly kisses and licks his way down the length of her body.

"Ice cream?"

"Yeah, ice cream. I want to see if you taste like ice cream, too." He reaches his destination and settles himself between her legs, at the juncture where her silky smooth thighs spread and separate, and allow him access to her liquid heat. He pushes his face down into her heated crevice, inhaling deeply and drawing in the distinctly musky, sweet scent of her sex. His tongue flicks and licks and laps and tastes the gathering pool of nectar, generated by his skillful touch.

"You taste like caramel, like caramel over ice cream," he whispers against her sensitive bud. "Mmm, you're so sweet. I can never get enough of your taste." He continues to stroke her silken walls with his tongue and to tease her hidden pearl; then he dips deep inside to taste more. She moans and writhes from the pleasure.

"Oh, babe, it feels so good, but I want to feel you inside me. I need to have your hard, throbbing cock here." She uses her hand to point the way. "Inside me now."

He shudders with desire and rises to fulfill her urgent plea. He pushes her legs higher, spreads them wider, moving into position to plunge deep. Her moans excite him and stir and push him toward the edge. He presses the tip of his shaft at her entrance, anxious and impatient to feel her hot, velvet sheath wrapped and squeezing tightly around his—

BEEP! BEEP! BEEP!

David's eyes flew open to the recognizable sound of the alarm clock incessantly beeping, the noise loud enough to wake the dead. He came fully awake, his body taut, rigid, and aching with a raging hard-on, his cock hard enough to punch through steel. Damn! It was another damn dream! He groaned and angrily slapped the off button on his clock. Closing his eyes and resting his head against the headboard, he tried to breathe through his painful erection, knowing the feeling would subside as the memory of the dream faded. Unable to completely quell the desire that constantly rode him, he punched the pillow in utter frustration: hard, hot, and achingly unfulfilled.

Chapter 1

Sunday

Sarona Maxwell waited patiently for her turn at the hotel registration desk. She'd just arrived at the end of a long day…tired, hungry, and ready for a meal and a hot shower. This was the final leg of a three-week business trip. The current endeavor was a five-day seminar of classroom instruction and vendors' exhibits showcasing software and peddling technology. Though her hectic travel schedule was nearly over, she dreaded yet another week of crowded venues, too-small hotel rooms, and too much drama that came with the close proximity of too many people and personalities. When one was employed by corporate America, drama was an everyday occurrence. She was accustomed to events like this, and since these meetings occurred often it was likely she'd see associates she'd met before in some other city, at some other meeting. Maybe, she chuckled to herself, just once she'd be spared the usual host of pompous, superficial characters who were permanent fixtures in the world of corporate soap operas.

As she waited, she looked over her surroundings and admired the remarkable architecture and décor the hotel offered, impressive by anyone's standards. The lobby was huge and sported a glass wall front at the entrance, the height of which spanned the first two floors. The high ceiling was supported by giant square pillars, trimmed in rich walnut with mirrors on all four sides that picked up and reflected activity in every direction. Enormous crystal chandeliers, marbled floors, plush carpeting, and staircases in wood and brass worked in concert to impress and convey opulent elegance. Large sculptures, paintings, and works of art purposefully placed throughout the great expanse created a museum-like quality. The rich brown, green, and burgundy hues implied a sense of simple sophistication.

"May I help you, ma'am?" The cheerful voice of the hotel clerk brought her attention back to the front desk

"Yes, thank you," Sarona replied and presented her identification for registration. While going through the normal check-in and verification process, the clerk began to frown and mutter unintelligible comments.

"Is there a problem?"

"No, ma'am, I don't believe so, but there's been a change in your reservation that I need to confirm."

"What kind of change?" she responded, exasperated and concerned there might be yet another complication to add to an exhausting day already filled with changes and complications.

"Oh, no, ma'am, it's nothing serious. It seems you've been upgraded because we're overbooked. You'll still receive the quoted rate, but a much better room for the price," the clerk said with a bright smile. After the day Sarona had had, she liked the sound of "much better." She completed and signed the necessary paperwork, and the clerk thanked her for her patience and wished her a pleasant stay. Sarona gathered her things and left in search of the elevator, tiredly dragging her luggage behind.

Once inside her room, Sarona suddenly realized how understated and inadequate the terms "upgraded" and "much better" were to describe the change in her accommodations. The room was a suite, a jaw-droppingly huge suite. The décor was significantly different from that of the hotel lobby. There were various shades of bright corals, pinks, blues, and greens, with plush pillows of all sizes scattered over a sofa and two chairs. The carpet, a beautiful, sandy beige color, was luxurious, soft, and thick. The seating area was accented with brass and glass coffee and end tables, each sporting elegant crystal lamps, all arranged facing a 42-inch, flat-screen television mounted on the opposite wall. There was a small kitchenette and wet bar, complete with bar stools in highly polished brown maple and fabric that matched the sofa and chairs. The entire room overlooked a breathtaking view seen through sliding glass doors that opened onto a small balcony. Small, tropical trees and potted plants were placed all about.

Sarona dropped her bags and hurried excitedly to see the rest of the suite. Inside the bedroom, an enormous king-size bed occupied the center of the room, big enough to fit at least three people comfortably. The same colorful décor of the main suite was repeated here. Off to one side, a small alcove contained a seating area consisting of a loveseat, table, and chair placed in front of a large window.

In a state of shock, she made her way to the bathroom. The tub, slightly elevated, was unbelievably large and deep, with several jet sprays positioned all around. There was a separate shower stall with showerheads on three walls and one overhead. Situated next to it was a toilet and bidet enclosed in their own room. In the middle of the room was a long, low, wooden bench. The image of lavish excess was completed by shining brass fixtures and mirrored walls that reached all the way to the ceiling at each end of the tub.

"Oh, my God," she whispered. Stunned and nearly speechless, she leaned against the wall. "Oh, my God."

Still trying to shake off the shock of her discovery, Sarona gathered up her suitcases and began to unpack. As a rule she usually packed light, but with so many destinations in so many weeks, she had extra luggage. Among her usual travel necessities there were three things she considered essential and never left home without: earplugs for unexpected noises that could ruin a good night's sleep, socks for her constantly cold feet, and her vibrator for…uh…

tension release. She chuckled at the memory of a long-ago comment to her friend Joyce during one of their "woman-to-woman"
conversations: "Girl, my vibrator is like American Express. I don't
leave home without it." Her decidedly kinky twist on the well-
known commercial had left them both bubbling with laughter.

Joyce Jeffers was Sarona's closest friend. They'd met four years
ago during one of life's quirky coincidences—at an airport while
waiting for a delayed flight. The two struck up a conversation
over a mutual weakness for designer shoes and handbags and soon
discovered they had more in common than the overdue flight
home. During that two-hour wait, they developed an instant
bond, which had blossomed into a relationship that had grown
and strengthened over time. Joyce was a few years older and wiser
and, as was expected with close friends, felt it was her duty to pass
on her personal and professional experience and opinion, whether
it was asked for or not. She fulfilled the prerequisite role of best
friend and confidante and listened, encouraged, persuaded, or
championed whenever called upon.

Sarona was an only child and had grown up isolated and alone,
separated from the rest of the world by strict and overprotective
parents. As a consequence of living a sheltered life, she was strong-
willed, independent, and had a mind of her own. The down side
was she often found it challenging to integrate herself into social
situations. It wasn't that she disliked being around people—she
disliked being around a *lot* of people, and unfortunately, her
preference for privacy and solitude threatened to turn her into a
recluse. She'd also discovered through experience that at times she
could be a bit naïve when it came to understanding people and
their motivations—another flaw she recognized and struggled to
overcome. She fought to keep a balance between her gullible and
accepting side and the other skeptical and suspicious side. For her,

it was a fine line to walk, and having Joyce as a friend and mentor helped make sense of the differences between the two.

Sarona finished putting her things away, and giving her suite another appreciative survey, stared longingly at the bed. Although she could easily have fallen face down into the enormous bed and not come up for air until the next day, she was unable to ignore the persistent hunger signals her stomach kept sending to her brain. So, before she gave into the exhaustion that threatened to claim her, she decided a quick visit to the hotel restaurant would solve at least one of her problems.

An hour later, with her hunger sated, she ended her long day with a glass of wine and a blissful soak in that absurdly large tub. And then, finally, sank into the welcoming softness of a king-sized bed, fit for a queen.

*

Monday

The seminar kicked off with its usual fanfare: preliminary introductions of directors, board members, and chair members, all taking turns giving their own personal welcoming speech. There was, of course, the extended invitation to meet fellow forum members in a more casual environment during the obligatory first evening mixer. A promise of free hors d'oeuvres, beverages, and cocktails was sure to guarantee maximum participation.

At the end of the day Sarona returned to her suite. Putting away her training materials, she was torn between returning for the mixer or staying in and ordering room service. As usual, she would have preferred to spend the evening alone reading, but if she didn't show up she'd spend the next day as the subject of good-natured teasing and being accused of anti-social behavior.

It wouldn't be far from the truth—she had very little interest in socializing and found it difficult to change a lifelong practice of avoiding the ritual. It was easier to avoid the circumstances altogether than to make token appearances. Giving a sigh of resignation and chalking it up to one of those necessary evils, she changed out of her business attire into something more casual, and left to join the group…just for a while.

*

David stood back and away from the crowd, secluded and cleverly hidden from view. A large sculpture and the branches of a strategically placed potted tree shielded his position. He resembled an animal stalking prey, his eyes constantly in motion, scanning and searching the room until he found what he was looking for.

"Sarona, there you are," he murmured. He watched as she mingled and moved about the room, stopping every few steps to engage in small talk with the others. He'd become quite adept at reading her, and he watched now as she slowly and steadily worked her way across the large room, edging toward the nearest exit to undoubtedly make her escape. He tracked her movements toward her intended route, hazarding a guess at how long it would take her to disappear altogether. That was her M.O.—make an appearance to show her face, socialize for a short period of time, and then move on before anyone noticed. But sometimes, if waylaid by a particularly persistent individual, her retreat could be delayed for hours, and that was what he was counting on.

He'd picked up on this habit and other interesting details after a number of months spent observing how she moved and interacted. He knew her, and he knew she was biding her time and planning her getaway. Well, he had news for her—tonight it wasn't going to be that simple. She was going to have to stick around a bit longer, if he had any say about it. Tonight, he had a vested interest.

Though they'd only met a few times in the past, he found himself totally intrigued and captivated with her personality; the fact she was beautiful was simply an added bonus. His curiosity had been piqued by her lack of interest in the usual superficial trappings or the need to impress. With his considerable experience in pursuing women, it was something he'd rarely seen, and he wanted to learn more. However, his attempts to get to know her better were met with complications at every turn. He was acutely aware that she put up a wall between them whenever he tried to initiate conversation.

Oh, she was nice enough, polite, even friendly, but he could detect that in some way she was put off by him, and avoided him every chance she got. He didn't think she liked him very much, and he didn't have a clue why, so he took a perverse pleasure in hunting her down and forcing her to tolerate his company. Even though his actions were precipitated by his adolescent-like behavior, he'd discovered that he enjoyed being with her whenever he got an opportunity. He found her smart and witty with an outrageously wicked and teasing sense of humor…whenever she slipped and let her guard down. Then he was allowed a glimpse at something deeper and beyond her distant polite exterior.

It was their last encounter and conversation, repeated over and over in his head, that had put him on edge and had unexpectedly triggered an obsessive need to get closer. Something she'd said had haunted him and pushed his mind and imagination beyond their limit for far too many days and nights since.

David had waited six months for this moment. He wasn't even supposed to be there, but he'd wangled an exchange of venue with a co-worker. He knew Sarona would be there because he'd made the necessary checks and inquiries to make certain of it. This five-day conference was going to be his ticket to getting closer to her and getting to know her—intimately. He was limited in what he could do in only five days. The short amount of time would be a stretch even for his ability to charm and persuade, but he was optimistic. He had confidence on his side. He'd worked his magic and gotten what he wanted in far less time, so this situation should be no different. He'd spent the last six months immersed in total fantasy. He had tortured his poor mind and body beyond endurance with vivid dreams and visions of her beautiful face contorted in sexual ecstasy, her imaginary soft moans of pleasure echoing in his head. He'd made up his mind six months ago. There would be no escape for her this time. She would not be allowed to ignore him or brush him aside as she had done repeatedly in the past. This time she was going to have to deal with him face-to-face, one on one. He had plans for her, plans he'd already taken the necessary steps to put into motion. Somewhere along the way she had become his obsession, and he was going to have her, seduce her into bed, his or hers—it didn't matter.

David knew he had a certain, perhaps unsavory, reputation and that it preceded him wherever he went. Tales told and spread among the women he had been intimate with over time had seen to that. He'd learned at an early age there was something about him, something to do with his biological chemical makeup along with his striking good looks that attracted the opposite sex in droves. As a young boy, he had thought it was a curse and hated the uncomfortable situations he had suffered through with little girls practically chasing him everywhere he went. But, by the time he'd hit puberty, he'd discovered the true advantage he had in the hand he'd been dealt, and well…the rest was history. Women were drawn to him like moths to a flame, vying for his attention and affection, and he willingly obliged, for he was, after all, merely a man.

He admitted he liked the attention, but over the last year or so he'd grown tired of the role. Everything was too easy. There was no challenge and no excitement, and the outcome was always the same, at least until he'd met Sarona Maxwell. Sarona was elusive, unobtainable, her manner remote, mysterious, and she seemed always just out of reach. Her elusive ways intrigued and challenged him, and were all the more reason why he had to have her. He believed Sarona was just what he needed to revive his interest in the pursuit of a beautiful woman, because *this* woman certainly didn't make anything easy. Her avoidance of him approached to the point of snobbery, and he refused to be snubbed.

He continued to watch her undetected, studying her from his concealed position.

No, she wasn't the type he was normally attracted to, but to tell the truth, he'd become pretty damned bored with the type he was normally attracted to. Sarona was black—or was that African American? He was never sure which term was politically correct. He guessed she was probably in her early to mid-thirties, but not much younger than his thirty-six years. She was above average height—tall for a woman and only a few inches shorter than his height of six feet three inches. She had a full figure with large breasts and luscious curves, perfectly proportioned in an hourglass shape reminiscent of those old Marilyn Monroe films his dad used to watch on late night TV. Her skin was the color of caramel, the kind you see drizzled over vanilla ice cream, and it looked just as rich, just as creamy. Her hair was a rich, dark brown with streaks of mahogany and fell in long, wild, and thick layers down her back to just below her shoulders. She had a warm, beautiful smile and intelligent, dark brown eyes, deep enough for a man to swim in…or drown trying. He was drawn to, aroused by, and turned on by her dark skin, dark eyes, and dark hair.

He shuddered and hardened at an unexpected visual: the two of them with their limbs intertwined against a backdrop of soft candlelight, champagne, and satin sheets. His lips locked against the softness of hers, his tongue delving deep, seeking to taste the sweetness of her mouth. His hand cupped the fullness of her breast, stroking her dark nipple with his thumb, pressing his hard arousal firmly against her, maneuvering and thrusting to get deep inside her waiting, wet...

"There you are!" The familiar sound of Shelia Preston's voice startled him and brought him reluctantly out of his fantasy. "Everyone's been looking all over for you and lucky me, I'm the one who's found you." She all but purred her satisfaction.

Of all people, David thought with bitter resentment he miraculously managed to keep from registering on his face. Shelia was a former lover who refused to be relegated to the classification of "former." She constantly sought him out with the intent to lure him back, but there wasn't a chance in hell of that ever happening. That time was long past. He conceded she was a beautiful woman; that's what had attracted him. She was ultra-feminine, blonde-haired and green-eyed with a willow-thin body envied by the world's average woman, topped with today's must-have accessory, thirty-four DD silicone breasts. Although she was great to look at and an ornamental showpiece for any man's arm, her personality was about as interesting as sitting around and watching paint dry. Thinking back, he wondered what in the world he could have seen in her in the first place. Of course, thinking back, he had to admit personality hadn't been his primary consideration. He probably hadn't bothered to raise his eyes above her neckline.

"Hey, anybody home in there?" Shelia yelled as she shook his arm, once again bringing him back to the here and now. "Come on." She dragged him forward. "I want to show everybody I found you." Looping her arm into the crook of his, she led him out into the crowded room, preening and strutting like she'd just won a blue ribbon for the prize bull at the County Fair—a role David suddenly realized he was becoming all too familiar with, and one that left him feeling more like a prize than a person.

*

Sarona stood off to the side of the large room watching the crowd mill about, the mass of people conversing and networking with one another. She'd already met a few individuals she was marginally acquainted with earlier in the day, but so far she hadn't seen even one of them here. That made her wonder why she'd bothered making an appearance.

As she sipped wine and surveyed the room and considered whether she should call it a night, her gaze suddenly fell upon a familiar figure on the far side of the room. She knew who he was instantly, even though all she could see was his backside. She'd recognize that backside anywhere.

"Damn," she muttered. The "he" who caught her attention was none other than David Broussard. David was an extremely attractive man who stood about six foot three with piercing whisky brown eyes that shimmered like a mixture of bourbon and honey, rimmed by sinfully long dark lashes that had no business being on a man. His hair was a cap of coffee-brown curls, full and springy yet perfectly styled, trimmed and tapered to the nape of his neck. His facial features were strong and squared with lush, full lips and a straight, patrician nose, giving an impression of chiseled perfection equal to that of the Greek god Adonis himself. Flawless, golden-bronze skin, a lean muscular frame with broad shoulders and a narrow waist that tapered into the nicest ass she'd ever seen, rounded out what could only be described as a perfect living example of God's gift to women. The man personified satin and silk, fire and ice, sex and sensuality, and the wine and candlelight she so wantonly desired. All told, he was a damn fine white man.

It was a well-known fact Mr. Broussard was a highly sought after, bona fide, honest-to-God ladies' man. His handsomeness would lend credence to such a claim, but it wasn't his looks alone that turned women's heads. There was something else about the man that could set a woman's senses on fire. He had a scent like no other, an actual natural scent that wafted into the air and drove women to nearly stampede like a herd of cattle.

The man's scent was to women like catnip was to cats—overpowering and irresistible. He could have any woman he wanted, and unfortunately, Sarona was no more immune to the natural power he wielded than any other member of the female sex. Knowing she was as susceptible as all the others, she did everything she could to stay off his radar and out of sight, but for some reason she couldn't fathom, every time she turned around, there he was.

The two of them had crossed paths off and on over the last year at venues like this, but had rarely engaged in what could be considered real conversation. They'd exchanged friendly flirtatious bantering, she teasing him about his reputation, he inviting her to explore the truth or myth of it for herself, but nothing more. She knew it was all just talk between them. She had no real concern he was actually interested in her, considering the obvious. She was black. She didn't fit his preferable parameters of attraction with her brown skin, full lips, big bust, and large, rounded bottom, all packaged in a daunting five-foot ten-inch frame. She was certain she had far too many curves for his taste. He'd once commented on her height and size and referred to her as an Amazon Queen. She silently chuckled, remembering the words they'd exchanged.

"That's right; I'm a *real* woman, so I suggest you save those Disneyland tactics you use for those anorexic, skin and bone-thin women you seem so fond of. If you step to me, you'd better bring it from the Wild Kingdom."

His eyes had grown wide with obvious surprise before he burst into a loud, boisterous laugh. She joined in, relieved that for once her habit of speaking first and thinking later hadn't landed her in hot water. Once the laughter died, he'd given her a curious look and responded in a much too intimate voice. "You know, Sarona, I'd be more than happy to go on safari with you any time. Just say the word."

She'd ignored his hint of implied interest because, for all her talk and bravado, there was no way in hell she was following him down that path. She'd told herself if there was any real interest, it was probably to satisfy the usual white man/black woman curiosity, and she'd be damned if she'd be seduced for the sake of curiosity. She'd seen and heard enough with her own eyes and ears to know any woman with half a brain and an ounce of self-preservation would steer clear of a man like him. She had no intention of getting mixed up in the games he liked to play.

She'd been around long enough to know that was all sex was to David—simply a game of stalk, capture, and conquer. "But damn." She sighed. "It sure is tempting to play."

She recognized the usual throng of women surrounding him, particularly the leader of the pack, Shelia Preston. Gossip had it David had recently dumped her after a brief fling, but the silly bitch didn't have sense enough to let go. Shelia mistakenly thought her good looks, fake boobs, and Daddy's money could get her any man she wanted. She thought material things entitled her to treat people with disrespect and allowed her the luxury of commanding the attention of any man, including David Broussard. Ordinarily that might have held true, but David Broussard wasn't just any man.

She had to admit, he was quite good at the hunt. Even now, while charming the women in front of him, he was scanning the room looking for his next target. By the look of determination on his face, he would have his next victim bagged and tagged in well under the five-day deadline. The man was lethal, and he looked every bit the predator he was.

She was *not* happy he was there, and her dismay at seeing him was testament to how she too was affected by his seductive persona. *God, the man's one big, walking pheromone,* she thought, disgusted with her irrepressible response to his presence.

Chapter 2

"So, David, I haven't seen you around lately. Where have you been keeping yourself?" Ellen Matthews inquired.

He remembered Ellen from events he'd attended in the past. He liked her. She was friendly, intelligent and down to earth. He was surprised to see her with Shelia. Most of the women in her circle of friends were a lot like her—vain, materialistic and totally unaware of the world outside their own personal social sphere.

"I've been busy starting up a new business venture."

"That sounds exciting. What kind of business is it?"

"It's software development with an emphasis on communications security. My partner and I have developed organizational software directed at major corporate businesses in need of standardizing their operations."

"Wow! That sounds like a lucrative venture."

"Yes, you're right. It's lucky for us there's a demand for what we offer. In this business, there are a lot of companies that compete and offer similar services, but fortunately we've developed something that's unique, smarter and simpler, at least for now."

"What corporate clients have you acquired? Anyone I may have heard of?"

"We've built up a modest clientele, but mainly work by referral since we have such a small staff. It keeps us busy, but as you can see, I haven't given up my day job yet." David chuckled as he took a sip from his drink.

"Oh, he's just being modest," Shelia interrupted. "Go ahead, David, tell her who you've done consulting work for."

"It's not important," he said, clearly uncomfortable with Shelia's entering into the conversation. "I don't want to bore Ellen with a laundry list of names that don't mean much."

"How can you say that?" She chuckled. "Of course they do. They're only some of the most recognizable names in the corporate world—names like Disney, Hilton, Jack in the Box...and those are just the ones *I* know about. With a list like that, his company could be on the Fortune 500 list in no time," Shelia blurted, obviously happy to tell such noteworthy news.

"Impressive," Ellen murmured.

Growing impatient with the company and the conversation around him, David took to searching the crowd again for Sarona. God, he hoped she hadn't left yet. He had to see her; he had talk to her. He was afraid being distracted by Shelia might have cost him his chance for the evening. Time was short—much too short. There were only a few days to get his plan to work, and he couldn't afford to miss one opportunity to corner her and make her notice him.

As luck would have it, he spotted her across the room at a tall, freestanding bar table, with a guy who looked totally absorbed in discussion with her. Seeing an opportunity in the making, he interrupted Shelia and her friends and politely excused himself, saying he'd just seen someone he wanted to chat with.

Shelia pouted her disappointment and tried to entice him to stay, shamelessly boosting the cleavage of her silicone breasts to their best advantage. David smiled distractedly and gave her a quick pat on the back, assuring her they'd talk later, and hurriedly walked away.

*

Shelia watched him leave and tried to follow his progress through the crowd, seething with anger. How dare he embarrass her in front of her friends? She knew he had some silly notion that they were suddenly just friends since *he* decided to call it quits, but if he thought he could drop her like all the others and just walk away, he was in for a rude awakening. He needed to be reminded they were two of a kind, and they belonged together.

David stopped at the bar to pick up a white wine and a shot of bourbon, neat. He'd noticed Sarona's glass was nearly empty. Though his objective was to show his good intentions and consideration, his good intentions were prompted by something more self-serving in nature. He was going to postpone her escape and charm his way into spending time with her for the evening. He was on a tight schedule, and he wouldn't let an empty glass be an excuse to call it a night, not yet. While waiting for the drinks and watching the interplay of conversation between her and her table mate, he tried to determine if she had any interest in the man in front of her.

Sarona was a remarkable woman when it came to intelligence, good looks, and charm, and he wasn't the only man enchanted by the seductive combination. He'd seen for himself the evidence of that as heads turned and bodies swiveled in unison when she walked by. Though she was a beautiful woman like Shelia, unlike Shelia, she didn't treat people as if compliments and admiration were her due. On the contrary, she didn't appear to even notice the attention she garnered by simply passing through. She exuded a certain sophistication, charm, and sexual attraction that were as natural as breathing, and she seemed totally unaware of it.

Even now he was captured by what he saw. She looked sexy as hell dressed in a colorful green, brown, and gold sleeveless, low-cut blouse that showed off her toned arms and ample cleavage. Camel brown slacks hugged her shapely behind and draped her long legs. Her toenails were polished, and her soft, elegant feet were sheathed in golden sandals. It was a given that the woman looked sexy in anything she wore, but at this moment, he literally ached for the opportunity to see her in absolutely nothing at all.

A sudden vision of her fully nude body stretched out like a sacrificial offering for his personal pleasure sent a rush of fire straight to his already throbbing cock, triggering his entire body to pulsate with intense desire. He imagined her chocolate-brown nipples standing taut, erect, begging to be stroked by his tongue, suckled and pulled into the warmth of his hot, eager mouth. He saw his hands skimming over her skin, the contrast of her creamy caramel and his sun-kissed bronze merging and blending, intermingling as he reached to cup her luscious hips and his fingers poised to stroke, probe, and explore the warmth of her mysterious depths...

The sound of her husky laughter brought David out of his daydream and replaced his dazed look with one of determination. With both glasses in hand, he made his way across the distance. He'd instantly decided two things—one, he didn't like the sound of Sarona's throaty laughter resonating with pleasure for someone else, and two, he didn't care who the man was, his time was up.

*

Sarona's planned retreat to her suite had been delayed by Bruce Carter, one of the regulars she vaguely knew. Uninvited, he had taken up residence at her table and was attempting to convince her tonight could be her lucky night. Bruce was just another married man away from home trying to score before going back to the wife and kids. She had no idea how she'd gotten his attention, but she had neither the interest nor the patience for his solicitation, and she hadn't been able to politely persuade him to move on.

"So, Sarona, what do you think? We're wasting time. How about we blow this place and go up to my room? We could have our own little party, just the two of us."

"You must be joking," she said, shocked at the suggestion and the assumption she was the least bit interested. She laughed out loud. "Why on earth would you think I'd be interested in going to bed with you?"

"Well, maybe you aren't right now, but if you give me a chance, I'm sure I could change your mind."

"Really," she responded dryly. "And how do you propose to do that?"

"Be persistent, wear you down, and if worse comes to worse, get you drunk. Look, a hot woman like you can have your pick of any man in this room. You can't blame a guy for trying to be the first in line. Time is short—we only have a couple of days—why not make the most of a great opportunity while we're away from home?"

"Because I don't need to 'make the most of a great opportunity.' I'm not the one who's married and searching for sex on the side with a restricted timetable."

"Okay, I'll give you that, but what's the harm in taking a walk on the wild side, especially since you have nothing at stake and nothing to lose? We're both just passing through. We get together for a night, two if we like it, then when it's over, go our separate ways."

This is just great, she thought with increasing annoyance. *He's certainly living up to his intention to be persistent; and making himself a pest to boot.* She was actually starting to get a headache. He didn't know it, but the man was coming dangerously close to making her lose her polite façade, meaning she was about to get ugly.

She did not want to resort to acting like an angry black woman, but he was working her last nerve.

She was still debating how to convince Bruce to give up and move on when she looked up and saw David striding purposefully toward them. His eyes met and held hers with a look of stubborn resolve. *Oh, hell,* she thought with exasperation, *just what I* don't *need right now.*

David sauntered up to her table with two glasses and, after giving a brief nod of acknowledgement to Bruce, he handed the wine to Sarona.

"Here, Sarona. I noticed your glass was nearly empty."

She was absolutely speechless, so she simply smiled and accepted the glass he offered. David turned to her table companion, stretched out his hand, and introduced himself.

"Hello, I'm David Broussard."

"Bruce Carter," the man said as he shook David's hand.

"Well, Bruce, I want to thank you for keeping Sarona company until I arrived, but she and I have some things to catch up on, and I'm afraid I'm going to have to steal her away from you." He turned to Sarona and added, "I'm sorry I'm late, but I was unavoidably detained and couldn't get away until now."

"Oh, that's all right, David," she said as she promptly jumped at the lifeline he'd thrown her. "Bruce was just about to leave anyway, weren't you, Bruce?"

Eyeing them both with a crafty smile, Bruce nodded his head in agreement and turned to walk away. In leaving, he commented over his shoulder, "I guess I can see now why you weren't interested in my proposal, Sarona. Obviously you were waiting for a better offer."

"Oh, no, Bruce, I'm afraid you're mistaken," she retorted. "It wasn't the proposal I had a problem with. I thought the presentation was unimpressive, unimaginative, and lacked sufficient substance to generate any interest."

Bruce, rendering a two-fingered salute, smirked as he departed.

"Snake!" she snapped as his back disappeared into the crowd.

"Looks like I got here just in time." David chuckled, raising his glass to his lips.

Sarona looked up to see sensual laughter sparkling in his eyes and thought with mild despair, *Oh, Lord. I've just traded the snake for a tiger.*

"So, David," she jokingly asked. "To what do I owe this honor? Don't tell me you've already stalked your way through the entire herd and decided to call it quits for the evening."

"I'm sorry to report that so far I haven't seen any decent prospects. But it's still early. I've got a few days to look them over before making a selection. But no matter the outcome, Sarona, I'll still have plenty of reserves left just for you—that is, if you're up for the hunt," he teasingly retorted.

"Ah, yes, the hunt." She laughed as she studied the wine in her glass. "I seem to recall an invitation to go on safari the last time we saw each other. However, after due deliberation, I've decided I'm in no way capable of competing at your level of expertise, so I think I'll be content to just sit back and watch an experienced master at work—watch how it's done, take a few notes," she remarked, lifting her gaze and her glass at the same time.

"Coward," he whispered.

"Exactly," she responded.

*

The two slipped seamlessly into the usual back-and-forth banter they'd come to share, as though no time had passed between their meetings. David once again played the game and eased effortlessly into his role of bad boy/player, a role he'd donned simply to get Sarona's attention and have her talk to him. He wasn't exactly thrilled with her perception of him, but if given the opportunity to set the record straight, he hoped to change that. He wanted her to see there was more to him than the playboy persona she was used to and so ready to believe.

He didn't like it, but he'd accepted the fact that for some unknown reason she wasn't susceptible to his male magnetism or glib charm. She either brushed aside his flirtatious advances or ignored him altogether. He couldn't decide if it was a blow to his male ego to be summarily dismissed, or if he was intrigued by the challenge. No matter the answer, he had to admit his desire intensified more and more each time he saw her and each time she rebuffed him. Surprisingly, each rejection only served to heighten his curiosity, and strengthen his resolve to get closer.

At his suggestion, they took their drinks and left the crowded room in search of quieter surroundings. They seated themselves in the bar and lounge area of the hotel.

"You know, David, considering how long we've known each other, it's occurred to me that we've never once discussed what you do. I'm curious. What brings you to these conferences? What *do* you do to make an honest living when you're not on the prowl?" she teased.

He smiled at her question. He secretly enjoyed knowing that, despite the fact they'd met on so few occasions, he knew more about her than she would ever suspect. He had reason to want to know everything he could; he needed an advantage, an edge. He was on a mission, a mission that had led him here to this moment. He was going to win her over, and he would use whatever recourse was available to him to ensure his success. If it meant lying and gathering information to the point of stalking, then so be it. He had no qualms or hesitations in using whatever means necessary when it came to getting what he wanted, and he wanted Sarona.

"I work for a communications security consultant firm. Our home base is in Atlanta, Georgia. I'm one of the consultants retained by the firm."

"Atlanta? That's where I'm from." Sarona responded with wide-eyed surprise.

"You don't say," David replied, the lack of real surprise evident in his voice. "I guess it really is a small world."

"Hmm," she said. "I have a feeling that you're not nearly as shocked as I am regarding this curious coincidence."

"No, I'm not surprised. I've overheard the conversations and gossip from the others when the subject comes up about who's attending these meetings. Whether you know it or not," he said with an impish sparkle in his eyes, "you, my friend, have been a hot topic of discussion on numerous occasions, with the emphasis on *hot*."

"Yeah, right!" She snorted a clear indication of her disbelief and laughed out loud at what she obviously considered a piece of fiction. "Please tell me why should I believe an outrageous comment like that?"

"Why would I lie?"

"To get my interest and draw me into your trap, that's why." She chuckled. "But I'm onto you, Mr. Broussard, and I'm not falling for it. I know you're a hunter, and you'll use any trick in the book to bait your intended prey, and I'm sure you'd use anything up to and including outrageous, pre-fabricated flattery. But, if you want to practice your lines and lies on me, go ahead. I'm game. I'm more than happy to give you constructive feedback."

"You think you know me, don't you, Sarona?" he asked, eyeing the contents of his glass speculatively. "You think you have me all figured out. You think I'm a man with no feelings and no heart, with one thought and one agenda—to pursue and capture. I think if you took a moment to put judgment aside and look deeper and beyond the façade, you might find something much more simple and unexpected. You might find that the hunter has a heart."

"I don't question whether you have a heart, David. I'm sure it takes a determined 'heart' to master the art of hunting. But hunters are a breed of their own, and by nature hunt for the sport, the competition, or the challenge. They are collectors of beautiful and unique things, whether purely for the sake of bragging rights, a sense of triumph or for other, more selfish reasons."

"And what category do I fall into, Sarona?" he asked, finding himself irritated and bothered to be so callously characterized.

"Umm…" She knitted her eyebrows together in the pretense of giving the question intense consideration. "Speaking strictly from observation, I'd say you're in it for the sport, because it's obvious there's no competition, and there's certainly no challenge."

Sarona's remarks made him uncomfortable. He found he didn't much like her opinion of him. Though the analogy of his being on the hunt had started as a joke, he was becoming concerned with her distorted view of him. Maybe it was time to change the subject. Steer her in another direction, into safer waters, until he had time to reconsider his approach. She was proving to be much more critical in her thinking than he'd originally assumed, and much too perceptive for his liking. He was going to have to re-examine his tactics and change his plan of attack.

"Well, enough about your decidedly unflattering opinion of me," David said, interjecting quiet laughter to segue into another, less intimidating topic. "How about you. Tell me more about what it is that you do."

"What?" she asked with eyebrows playfully raised. "Don't tell me an observant and discerning man such as you didn't acquire that all-important bit of information from those overheard discussions about how hot I am!

They both burst into companionable laughter at her jab, and the conversation and the evening went on from there. Quips, conspiracies, and scandalous commentaries between the two continued throughout the night, interspersed with reactions from sedate chuckles to riotous laughter. The topics of conversation ranged from politics to business, to food and wine, to music and movies, and covered a broad spectrum of personal opinions, beliefs, likes, and dislikes.

During the evening, David learned of Sarona's schedule when she indicated she'd be leaving early Saturday morning. He made a mental note that, including tonight, he had five nights to accomplish his goal.

*

At a comfortable lull in the conversation, David excused himself to order more drinks, leaving Sarona alone with her thoughts. With chin in hand and watching people passing by, she idly speculated about David. Why was he spending so much time with her? She was baffled by his persistence in seeking her out everywhere they went. Considering his womanizing reputation, he should be out scouting for potential bed partners, not wasting his time chatting it up with her. She had to wonder if there were some other purpose behind his unusual behavior. Men like David simply did not hang out with women like her for the sake of company and conversation. There had to be a reason, some motive.

Motive?

Sarona's eyes widened with sudden revelation. *Stupid woman, of course there's a motive! Sex! Holy crap, he's actually* serious! *The man's got it in his head that he wants to have sex with you! And all this time you thought he was simply joking. How could you not see this coming?*

How?

Because you were too busy being smug, thinking it was all fun and games and that you weren't his type. Hell, anything with two legs and female would be his type. Damn!

"*Now* what are you going to do," she muttered to herself.

Run! her inner voice of reason shouted.

*

Shelia stood with the crowd, feigning interest in the chatter going on around her, but her eyes were on David and Sarona, and she was upset with what she saw. *What the hell is he doing? He can't possibly be interested in her! Look at her, she's huge! She's a cow!* She'd been trying desperately to get David to come to his senses and come back to her.

Her phone calls and messages had gone unanswered. When they did speak, the conversation was clipped and cut short, not that they had ever talked much, anyway. Shelia didn't have much use for conversation; she thought it was a waste of time. What she wanted most was his attention, and of course, sex. The sex was great! She'd never in her life experienced anything like the pleasure David gave her. She'd finally met a man who knew exactly what he was doing in bed, and there was no way in hell she was letting him get away. She had no idea what had gone wrong or why he'd suddenly lost interest, but she'd invested a lot of time and energy into getting him, and she wasn't giving him up, not without a fight.

Her eyes narrowed to slits as she watched the two of them. Hearing the laughter and watching the smiles and looks that passed between them only made her angrier. Unable to stomach another moment of watching them together, Shelia turned and rudely pushed through the crowd as she made her way toward the elevators.

"What's her problem?" Linda asked, watching Shelia's sudden and unexplained departure.

Ellen chuckled at the sight of Shelia's stiff back in retreat. "It looks like Shelia's got competition, and she doesn't like it one bit."

"Competition?" Linda murmured, following the direction of Ellen's gaze. "I thought they were over and done."

"As far as he's concerned they are, but as usual, Shelia has a problem facing reality."

"She doesn't let go easily, does she?"

"No, she doesn't. Shelia has the misconception that the world revolves around her, and she should be worshipped accordingly."

"Well, she is a beautiful woman," Linda stated in awe, reflecting too closely the worship Shelia was accustomed to.

"Oh, please! Of course she's beautiful. She's had so much work done, she's like the city of Las Vegas, constantly under construction." Ellen couldn't refrain from laughing at her own clever correlation, referencing Shelia's history of cosmetic maintenance. "These days there are more and more men opting for the experience of a natural woman. It would seem that Mr. Broussard is no exception."

"Do you think there's anything going on between those two?"

"I don't know, but from where I'm standing I'd say that the road they're on is bound to lead them somewhere."

Chapter 3

They stood at the door to her suite, still engaging in the back-and-forth banter they had participated in most of the evening. This was by far the most fun David had had in a very long time. It was rare to spend this much time with her, so he relished the moment, reluctant for it to end. Though he'd kept up his end of the conversation throughout the night, there were times he was barely aware of what had been said. More than once he'd found himself fascinated with Sarona's mouth, watching the way it moved when she spoke and the sexy way her tongue slipped out to moisten her lips. Other times he caught himself staring into her eyes, dazed and free falling into their darkness, drowning in their depths.

"Thank you for rescuing me from Bruce," he heard her say as she reached for her card key. "I wasn't having any luck convincing him to leave."

"No problem. I could tell he was making a jerk of himself by the way you were rubbing the side of your head. I might have left it alone, but you looked annoyed. I don't like seeing you annoyed," he said. "He didn't seem like your type so I had no qualms butting in and scaring him off."

"My type? What do you mean 'my type'?" she queried with raised eyebrows and a half smile that flitted across her face. "What exactly does 'my type' look like?"

"Like me," he stated without hesitation.

Sarona tensed, sensing the change in direction the conversation was about to take. "Well, I suggest you think again, Mr. Broussard." Her voice was edged with forced lightness. "You, sir, are way out of my league, but unlike most of the women you usually entertain yourself with, I'm smart enough to know it. I know the rules of the game, David," she responded with a smile that didn't quite reach her eyes, "but I'm not interested in playing."

David stepped back and clutched his hands to his heart in mock dismay, with what he hoped was a disarming smile. "You wound me deeply, woman, with your constant distrust. Can't a guy simply profess adoration without having an ulterior motive?"

She eyed him suspiciously and gave an unladylike snort. "Of course there's an ulterior motive…you're a man, aren't you?" She gave him her sweetest smile and cheerfully said, "Good night, David, thank you for a lovely evening," and entered her suite and closed the door in his face.

The smile slipped from his face like melting wax, to be replaced by a look of lost and utter confusion. For one fraction of a second, he didn't know what to think. What had just happened here? One minute they were engaging in playful repartee and the next—the next he was left standing in an empty hallway, alone! Suddenly, the improbable dawned on him. *I've been dismissed.* The realization was slow in coming. His reaction was stunned disbelief. He knew the woman was full of surprises, but this was one surprise he sure as hell hadn't counted on. David turned abruptly and stalked back down the hall to the elevator, his short-lived euphoria fast becoming a distant memory.

*

Sarona stood with her back to the door listening to his receding footsteps, muffled by the carpeting in the hallway. As the muted sound of the elevator arriving reached her ears, she pushed away from the door and headed to the bathroom. Staring back at her reflection in the mirror above the sink, she replayed the events of the evening in her head and examined the hours she'd spent with David.

The brush-off at the door had been nothing more than an act of self-preservation. It was a meager attempt to discourage his interest, and one that was sure to backfire. But if she were honest, she'd admit she'd had a wonderful time. And as long as she was being honest, she might as well admit that no matter how she tried to fight it, she was extremely attracted to the man.

God help her, she was as susceptible as every other red-blooded female within a fifty-foot radius to his alluring personality, that amazing scent, and his drop dead gorgeous good looks. She'd been captivated by his beautiful eyes and had loved watching how they'd sparkled with mischief and merriment when the conversation invariably turned to sexual innuendo. His smile was intriguing, followed often by an infectious laugh, the sound of which bordered wickedly on girl-go-ahead-and-drop-your-drawers-now sexy. To her surprise, he was a fun guy to be with. He was intelligent, charming, and funny. Despite the fact that he was capable of pouring on the charm and charisma to captivate and spellbind any woman alive, she had the feeling that instead he'd relaxed and let himself go, and enjoyed the evening as much as she had.

Hours later and still trying vainly to put the evening behind her, Sarona was wide awake, tossing and turning. Romantic thoughts of David ran rampant through her mind, closely followed by unexpected and unwanted heated responses from her traitorous body. Before tonight she hadn't given him more than a passing thought of interest, but now she couldn't get him out of her head.

Damn him! He'd charmed and teased her and made her laugh and had gotten under her skin like an annoying itch she couldn't reach or scratch. They'd only spent one evening together. How could one evening have such an effect on her? Suddenly her mind was in chaos and her body was on fire with a scorching desire that until now had barely existed. She couldn't keep the vision of his face, his eyes, and that sinful mouth—perfect, beautiful, and delicious—from flashing before her eyes. It should be against the law to look that gorgeous, to be that sexy. It was a lethal combination and a deadly distraction for average folk like her.

As a matter of fact, it would be better for womankind everywhere if he wore a warning label that said "Caution, Proceed at Your Own Risk." At least a girl would have some idea what she was in for. "The man should be registered," she mumbled to herself, irritated with where her thoughts continued to take her.

Ultimately, unable to push him back into obscurity where he belonged, she had no choice but to give up and give in to her now awakened and unrequited needs—needs she could no longer ignore or deny. She needed to feel the touch of a man's hands on her body, insistent and demanding. She needed to feel the brush of full, sensual lips, tempting and inviting, delivering long, deep, and drugging kisses.

She needed to feel the long, hard length of a man pressed intimately against her hot and waiting divide, pulsing, pushing and persistent. No longer able to resist her inner calling for relief she let go and fell forward into her own private world of imagery and imagination, wrapping herself inside a gossamer shroud of sexual fantasies.

She imagined his handsome face hovering inches from her own as she stared into amber eyes, dark and smoldering with intense desire. She felt his hands softly caressing her body, his fingers skimming, stroking her curves, gripping her cheeks, delving within her depths, and teasing and tweaking her taut bare nipples, and her mind took her farther and deeper into the fantasy.

She felt the brush of his curls rub against her breasts, tease her stomach, and torment her inner thighs as his hands kneaded and fondled her body. The touch of his lips and the thrust of his tongue seared and burned her skin as his heated mouth slowly made its way lower, licking, sucking, and tasting every inch. Her extended nub of flesh, firm and protruding, anticipated the hot, silken stroke of his tongue.

Her nipples hardened to the point of pain. Her breath quickened and her heart raced, as she was inescapably caught up in her perfectly contrived web of passion and seduction. A moan escaped her lips, and her own hands took on the role of imagined masculine exploration. She brushed and rubbed her clit and separated her lips; her fingers entered her hot, wet channel, plunged in and out, and moved back and forth at a frantic, frenzied pace. Her body responded, bucking, stretching, and reaching for release.

Try as she might, her imagination and manipulations simply weren't enough. She wanted more, needed more. Dammit! What she needed, she thought in exasperation, was the real thing. Dissatisfied, her body awash with frustration, Sarona reached inside the drawer of the nightstand and pulled out her number one essential item. With the flick of a switch, she disrupted the silence of the night with the unmistakable whispering whir of electronic vibrations.

*

David entered his suite and angrily snatched off his blazer and threw it across the room, watching it miss the mark completely and land on the floor. "Stupid! Stupid! Stupid!" he angrily berated himself. How could he be so stupid? He knew damn well she was wary of him—how could he make such a mistake? He should never have made that comment. As soon as it was out of his mouth, her entire attitude changed, and she put the brakes on so fast he felt like he had whiplash. The drop in temperature happened so quickly, he seriously thought that maybe he should check his extremities for frostbite.

He needed to think, and to think, he needed a drink. He walked over to the bar and poured himself a double shot of Hennessey. He turned on the radio, dialed in the local jazz station and adjusted the volume. Taking his glass and moving toward the balcony, he stopped to remove his shoes and socks and absently allowed his toes to stretch and curl into the softness of the plush carpet.

He opened the sliding glass doors and breathed deep, trying to clear his head. Staring out at the blinking city lights below and sipping his drink, David tried to regroup and formulate a plan. He needed a strategy to get past Sarona's defenses and get her where he wanted her—into his bed. Tonight's unexpected turn of events might be cause for concern, but he couldn't let it discourage him. *It's just a minor setback*, he told himself. Setbacks could be overcome, but the stakes had been raised. This was no longer a challenge or question of *if*. It was merely a matter of *when*.

After spending the entire evening absorbed in conversation and surrounded by her presence, he was more obsessed now than ever before. There was no way he was leaving this place without experiencing more of her. He had to have her because his body burned and ached from needing her. He had to touch, stroke, and taste her and uncover every intimate detail. Something dark and needy deep within him had to know if she tasted as sweet as that caramel drizzled over vanilla ice cream fantasy he couldn't erase from his mind.

Still unyielding in his determination, he set aside his drink, turned off the lights, and shed the remainder of his clothing, throwing them across a nearby chair. The room, dimly lit by lighting from buildings nearby, the street lights below, and the now and again flash of passing headlights, became the backdrop of his painfully persistent dance with want, need, and desire.

He stood fully nude before the large glass window, his mind filled entirely with a vision of Sarona. His hands slid down his body, tracing the ridges of his impressively toned and muscled chest and abdomen. His leisurely exploration stopped at his groin where he gripped his already hardening cock and began a slow, massaging stroke. He closed his eyes and allowed the sweet, sensual sound of the music to wash over him, surround him, and wrap him up in its seductive spell. And his mind slipped and fell into fantasy, drawing on what he knew for certain and everything he imagined…and with mind, hope, and passion, he reached for her.

Every detail, every shapely curve, slope and hollow—even that quirky, annoyed look she sometimes gave him—was emblazoned in his head. Her luscious body lay before him, the soft, rich brown of her skin in stark contrast to the bone-white satin sheets. Her hair was draped around her face and shoulders, creating a sensual, silky curtain of seduction; her deep brown eyes sexy and sultry; and her moist, succulent lips, slightly open, demanding to be kissed and devoured. With his virtual fantasy of breasts, curves, lips, eyes, and beautiful brown skin firmly etched in his mind, he leaned forward, legs spread apart, with one hand splayed on the glass and the other firmly wrapped around his shaft and let his imagination take him. He allowed it to lift him higher to bring him closer to deliverance from his constant state of want, arousal, and sexual frustration.

His hand stroked his shaft in a steady, up-down rhythm, twisting on the downward stroke. He gripped and teased his sac, sending short bursts of pleasure spiraling up into his stomach and down his thighs, to return and center in his groin. The sensation was an almost unbearable ache that left him balancing on the thin line between pleasure and pain. His skilled and practiced hand brought him so close to letting go; he could feel the threatening eruption of surging, pearly white cream, churning and pushing its way to the surface.

Reaching the edge came much quicker these days, but he had no intention of crossing over and bringing himself to climax. He wanted to savor the feeling, endure the pain and make it last. He refused to give in and let go until he found himself inevitably buried balls-deep inside his one and only passionate obsession, Sarona Maxwell. Denying himself had become a form of torture he endured, taking himself to the edge, teetering but never going over. He made himself wait, envisioning and anticipating how relief would be just that much sweeter once he found himself sheathed and surrounded by her wet, velvet softness.

Breathing deeply to ease himself back from the edge, he slowly released his grip on his cock and waited for the feeling of near euphoria to subside. He groaned and pulled himself out of his fantasy and back from the brink of madness. Shaking his head, he rubbed his face and sullenly thought what sweet, torturous pleasure it was to give in to the power of imagination, and reaching for his glass he stared out into the dark of night—naked, vulnerable and achingly alone.

He'd worked hard at being a success, and he'd succeeded in both his public and private life. But for all he'd done and all he'd gained, he found himself thinking more and more on what was missing. He admitted his reputation as a womanizer was true and well deserved. He made no excuses or apologies for that; it was the life he'd lived. However, contrary to what Sarona and the others might believe, his womanizing days had all but come to a screeching halt. He hadn't been with a woman in nearly a year. Ten months, twenty-three days, to be exact.

He'd kept up the appearance of being on the hunt because it staved off boredom and he knew it was expected, but he'd grown tired of keeping up appearances. He'd made a conscious decision to step back from engaging in random, unfulfilling sex, simply for the thrill and the conquest. But, somewhere along the line between his intentions and his libido, Ms. Maxwell had moved in and taken up residence in his subconscious, and suddenly his sexual fantasy control switch was permanently stuck in the *on* position. How it happened he couldn't say. All he knew was that she now reigned over his every thought and action, and the interminable wait to possess her was causing him to lose what little control he had left.

He was still contemplating his dilemma with Sarona when the ringing of the phone brought him out of his brooding state.

"Hello?"

"Hey man, it's Brice. What's up?"

"Hey Brice, how's it going?"

"Oh, pretty much the same old thing on this end. What about you? How's it going there? Learn any new and exciting revelations in the world of high-tech operations to keep us in step with the competition?"

"No, no such luck. So far they haven't shown me a thing we don't already know. As a matter of fact, we're so far ahead of these guys, maybe *I* should be teaching the class," he replied with a laugh.

"Yeah, I thought so." Brice chuckled. "The reason I called was to give you an update on our latest project. I have an appointment tomorrow morning at ten A.M. to make our pitch to that potential new client. I've done my homework, looked at their problem areas and weaknesses, and assessed their needs. I think we have a lot to offer in the way of streamlining their communications capabilities and upgrading their security."

"That's great news."

"It sure is. I thought it might be something worth passing on, especially since you're there making such a sacrifice and taking one for the team." He laughed out loud. "What about you? How are things shaping up with your personal agenda? Have you run into your Amazon Queen yet? How's the plan coming to charm and capture?"

Brice Coleman was not only David's business partner, but his best friend as well. They'd known each other since their college days and had recently embarked upon a business venture together. Both men worked for other companies, but the fact was, neither needed to work at all. They each came from wealthy families and had enough money to live the unencumbered lives of jet setters and world travelers. But neither man cared to live life idly without a sense of accomplishment or purpose. That was why, after several late night discussions over beer and pizza, they decided to branch out into business together. They wanted the challenge that owning and working a business would bring—something in which they had invested their own blood, sweat and tears. So, after endless discussions and debates, they finally came up with the concept for the company Security Matters.

David had told him everything, including his latest obsession with a certain dark-skinned beauty who seemed to constantly run naked through his mind. Brice had found himself fascinated and intrigued with his friend's out-of-character and unexpected attraction, bordering on obsession, with Sarona Maxwell. He knew every single dirty detail of David's bone-deep lust for women in general and Sarona Maxwell in particular. In fact, during their many male bonding sessions when drinking and discussing sports, sex, and women they often joked about the male gender's driving need to "divide and conquer," the phrase a metaphor used to refer to dividing a woman's legs and conquering her sexually.

David briefly went over the events of the evening in his head, and wasn't exactly sure how to respond to the question. "The night started out pretty well—actually better than I expected. I'd made some major progress until the evening took an unexpected detour and headed south. As usual, I had to force her to notice me, but this time I did it with flair. This time, she was a damsel in distress and I was her knight in shining armor."

"What the hell is that supposed to mean?"

"It means she was being harassed by some jerk trying to get into her underwear. I scared him off."

"Only to replace him with another jerk trying to get into her underwear," Brice gibed.

"Yeah, well, I've had my eyes on that underwear a lot longer than he has. I've invested considerable time and fantasy toward the prospect—too much to let some *other* jerk move in and reap the benefits."

"Maybe she's not interested?"

"What's not to be interested in?" David's voice was tinged with arrogance. "I'm tall, good looking, and I have a great body—and I smell good too. I repeat, what's not to be interested in?"

"You forgot to add your humility and overwhelming sense of modesty," Brice retorted sarcastically. "You know, man, maybe there's one woman in the world that the famous Broussard charm and pheromones don't work on. Think about it. It was bound to happen. You've had it too easy for too long. Out of all the years I've known you, you've never once had to work for sex. You and I both know that women line up to throw themselves *and* their underwear at you. Maybe this is nature's way of returning the balance to the rest of us poor saps who have to beg for or buy a woman's attention or sexual favors. I believe I speak for all of those less fortunate when I say, 'Welcome to our world!'"

"Don't be ridiculous," David grumbled, trying hard not to consider that there might be some shred of truth in what Brice said. "I just need to use a bit more finesse than usual. Sarona is not your average woman, and my average methods of seduction don't work with her. That's what fascinates me about her. Besides the fact she's sexy as hell, she's damned full of surprises too. She actually seems to have built-in bullshit radar."

"Yeah, right," Brice interrupted. "Before you go on and on again about how exceptionally hot you think Sarona is, you said you 'thought' you'd made progress tonight. What happened?"

"What happened was that we had the makings of a great evening together, and things were going fine, until I said something stupid. I could actually tell by the look in her eyes that I'd messed up. She literally shut the door in my face so fast, I'm lucky to still have my nose attached."

"What did you say?"

"It doesn't matter what I said. What matters is that this time I made it as far as her door before she ditched me. I was pretty damn angry at first, but now that I think about it, the evening wasn't a total loss after all. I actually got closer than I've ever been before."

Chapter 4

Tuesday

This day would probably go down in David's personal record book as the longest day in history. He'd been unable to speak to Sarona at all, not even a brief hello. They weren't attending the same sessions, so any glimpse he managed between breaks was a stroke of luck. When he did see her, her wary reaction told him last night's door in the face had set him back at square one. She was avoiding him again.

Sitting in his afternoon session, David was preoccupied and totally oblivious to the speaker. His thoughts were on Sarona, wondering what the heck was going through that mind of hers. He was both annoyed and angry—annoyed at Sarona for showing signs of a change of heart, and angry at himself for being responsible for that change. He'd done something to put her off. His instincts told him it wasn't entirely because of the comment at her door; there was more to it than that. He wasn't blind. There had always been an invisible barrier erected between them that only permitted him to get so close. Considering his reputation and his true purpose, she had every right to be wary, and every reason for the barrier. But, given his true purpose and his time constraints, he'd only respect her barrier for so long. His tolerance of her skittish behavior was quickly wearing thin.

Replaying the previous evening in his head, he knew there'd been a difference. She'd been relaxed and laid-back, just going with the flow. He told himself she'd enjoyed his company and the time as much as he had. He'd felt he'd made such progress in getting to know her better, and she in getting to know him, moving their friendship forward to the next level. But now, he was at a loss. He didn't know what had happened to suddenly change the rhythm of the evening. If the door in his face was the beginning, and today was further warning of things to come then his work was cut out for him. He was going to have to work extra hard to regain the precious ground he'd lost.

*

David sat in the back of the lounge, seated at the perfect vantage point to watch the passersby, yet remain virtually unde-tected. It was six o'clock in the evening and the bar was filling up, quickly nearing capacity. Happy hour was in full swing. Linger-ing over his drink, taking slow, easy sips, he casually surveyed his surroundings. His eyes scanned the area carefully, hopeful for a glimpse of caramel silk, hopeful Sarona might decide to put in an appearance. His façade was deceptively relaxed and casual; his mood was anything but.

He saw Shelia enter the lounge, and his hand tightened around his drink in agitation. He knew the exact moment she found him. Simultaneously, a sly, solicitous smile settled upon her lips, and a sparkle of triumph lit her eyes. He watched her glide toward him in long, sensual strides of feline grace, the practiced swing of her arms and the sway of her hips perfect, feminine, and elegant. He wit-nessed the predictable reactions as she breezed through the crowd, watching heads turn in accord and eyes fill with admiration and speculation. But it was all wasted effort on him, for he was no lon-ger impressed by or interested in Shelia's looks. He sighed audibly as she approached, steeling himself for what was sure to come— another meaningless diatribe on life according to Shelia.

"David, darling, how are you?" she cooed as she eyed the vacant chair next to him. "I'm so glad you have a table, it's so crowded in here." She raised her voice to be heard over the din. She didn't wait for an answer or an invitation. Assuming, as was her way, that it was perfectly all right, she seated herself and waved to get the attention of a passing waitress to order a drink.

Unfortunately, the woman didn't move fast enough and ended up on the receiving end of some pretty harsh words from Shelia's shrewish tongue. "Can you move any slower? A person could die of thirst waiting for service."

The apologetic waitress took her order and hurried away. David's eyes sympathetically followed the woman before he turned back to Shelia. It suddenly occurred to him that he'd often ignored Shelia's totally self-absorbed and impolite behavior. And, if he'd ignored it before, what did that say about him and the kind of man he was? Once again he asked himself what he had ever seen in this woman. *It's no wonder Sarona has such a dim view of me,* he thought. After taking a closer look at what Shelia represented as his taste in women, what else could she think?

David took to scanning the room again, mildly distracted by the droning sound of Shelia's voice. He was brought out of his roaming state when he became conscious she'd invited others to join them. To his surprise, suddenly there were three additional ladies preparing to occupy the remaining seats at his table. He stood and smiled in what he hoped was a warm greeting, but deep inside he was fuming. Why did Shelia need an entourage to accompany her everywhere she went? Had he overlooked that as well?

While helping the ladies to be seated he looked up, and was rewarded with the unexpected sight of Sarona as she entered the bar, flanked by a small group. His immediate response was elation; she had appeared after all, beyond his greatest expectations. His belated second response was pure, primal male jealousy, as his eyes registered the man standing next to her, his hand at her back and his attitude possessive.

*

Sarona entered the bar hesitantly, having agreed to come along only after repeated pressure from her friends. She'd had strong intentions to stay in her room for the evening and every night to come. She was determined to avoid even the slightest possibility of running into David.

She'd been lucky so far; she'd managed to dodge him the entire day. After suffering through one very long night of his invasion of her every waking *and* sleeping moment, she'd made up her mind to avoid him for the remainder of the week. If she had no defense against her own feelings and imagination, what could she possibly do against the power of his attraction up close and personal? She'd felt a twinge of guilt at the look of confusion and question in his eyes every time she'd seen his face throughout the day. But she couldn't afford to let guilt sway her resolve. This was a matter of self-preservation and keeping her wits about her. David was more than capable of affecting her senses...and making her witless. Maybe her luck would hold. It was a big place.

There were six of them, three women and three men, essentially paired off into couples. Thomas Khan had appointed himself as her escort for the evening. Thomas was a fine brother, handsome, tall, and lean with beautiful, flawless, rich chocolate-brown skin and surprisingly piercing hazel eyes. His hair was waved and cropped close to his head and lined to perfection, with sideburns that blended straight down his face into a meticulously trimmed mustache and goatee. Though his frame was lean, he had a tight, muscular build, as evidenced by the form-fitting muscle shirt and snug jeans he wore to show off his body. She and Thomas were in the same classes for the week, along with most of the others in the group. She'd reluctantly agreed to the invitation for drinks when she would much rather have stayed in her suite and enjoyed a long, hot soak in that ridiculously large tub.

Thomas took his voluntary role of escort seriously and acted as though he thought they were actually on a date. Sarona was a little concerned, but didn't want to read more into the situation than it warranted...and she hoped he didn't either. But as the evening wore on, she began to have her doubts. Throughout the night, she found herself constantly removing his hands from around her shoulder or slapping them as he rubbed across her thigh. He was continuously touching, rubbing, and taking liberties, and she found it exhausting trying to keep pace with his wandering hands.

Becoming increasingly annoyed with his behavior, she decided she needed to get away before she lost her temper and made a scene, so she excused herself to go to the ladies' room. The other women seized the opportunity and got up to join her.

*

David felt trapped. Thanks to Shelia, he'd been pressed into the role of reluctant host to a table full of uninvited guests. He'd admit there was once a time when being surrounded by a bevy of beautiful women might have been a boost to his ego, but not now, and certainly not tonight. Tonight, he was tremendously annoyed with the intrusion on his personal time and space. In search of a reason to escape, he made a quick survey of the table and decided they all could use a refill on their drinks. They hadn't seen the waitress in the last half hour so he used the dwindling drinks as an excuse to get away.

When he reached the bar, he placed his order and then set about searching the crowd for Sarona and her group. When he found her, his groin tightened with immediate recognition and need, and he instantly accepted and embraced the feeling. His body welcomed the automatic response of warmth and fire as his eyes roamed her face and body.

The jealous and possessive male in him rose to the surface when he got a closer look at the man by her side. Was he her date? He didn't like the thought of that. He'd never seen him before but clearly recognized the familiar signs of a man staking his claim. He showed all the signs of a man anticipating what was to come after drinks and conversation.

Was there something going on here that could affect his plans? Could everything he'd been working toward for the last six months be in jeopardy because of this man? He considered the ramifications as he studied the couple while waiting for his order. A closer look caused his eyes to narrow in concern; his jaw clenched, and his hands tightened into fists. It was plain to see she was uncomfortable and none too happy. The man was aggressive and pushy.

He was practically manhandling her, in plain sight! For one tense moment, he seriously considered walking right up to their table and snatching the guy by his collar and tossing him out of the bar. "Yeah," he mumbled under his breath, "and that would get me tossed out right behind him."

Sarona and the other women got up to leave the table and, seeing his chance, David took advantage of the opportunity to move closer and eavesdrop on the ensuing conversation. He learned the man's name was Thomas. David's stomach churned at the lustful look and smug smile upon his face as the guy watched Sarona move through the crowd. As he listened to the conversation between the men, he found their discussion equally unsettling.

*

"Man," Thomas said, "I can't wait to get Sarona behind closed doors. I can tell by looking at her that she's a real freak between the sheets."

Carl's head whipped around as he gave Thomas a look of utter shock and disbelief. "What the hell are you talking about? Man, you won't even make it to the door with that one. Sarona isn't the kind of woman who can be talked into anything, let alone into bed. Hell, it was like pulling teeth to get her to agree to come out with us tonight."

"I don't plan to do a lot of talking." Thomas slyly smirked and winked.

"Look, man, if I were you, I'd think twice before doing something stupid that might get me chopped off at the knees. I know a couple of other guys who invited her out to dinner with the same idea in mind, and from what I heard, she shot them down between the entrée and the dessert."

"Those other guys didn't know what they were doing," Thomas said, beginning to get annoyed with Carl. "All I need to do is get these soft lips and this magic tongue within striking distance, and that's all she wrote."

"And how do you plan to do that? From what I've seen, she doesn't want any part of you. She's been checking you and batting you away like a baseball player at spring training."

"That's just a minor technicality. She's probably playing hard to get because of you guys. Right now, I'm just feeling her out."

"You're 'just feeling her out'? Buddy, I don't know what kind of sign you're looking for but I'd say it looks like a pretty solid 'no, not interested' to me."

"I don't know, man," Michael interjected. "Maybe you should chill out and forget whatever it is you're planning. Sarona doesn't look like the kind of woman who'll put up with being mauled by her date for long."

"Who's talking about mauling anybody? Believe me, it'll be a whole different story once we get away from you guys. I'm telling you, it's just a game women like to play. Look, I know the score, and I've got a perfect record with the ladies to prove it. I haven't been told no yet," Thomas boasted.

"Well, there's a first time for everything," Carl mumbled into his glass, as he watched the three women returning to the table.

*

The dialogue was pretty much what David had expected, but still, it infuriated him to hear Thomas voice his intentions. He reluctantly admitted he was a good looking guy, and that being black could be something in his favor, but he decided the man didn't have a clue how to handle a real, genuine classy woman like Sarona. And Sarona was pure class; not your average, run-of-the-mill beauty who was all body and no brains. The two men at the table echoed his sentiments when they questioned Thomas about the feasibility of his plan. If he hadn't been so upset, he might have thought the situation comical. He was out of his league, and the poor sap didn't even know it. Looking up in time to see the ladies returning, David hastened to slip out of sight and back to the bar. He decided it was best not to be seen. Right now, the last thing he wanted was a face-to-face with Sarona.

He picked up the drinks and reluctantly returned to his table to rejoin the group. Tuning out the laughter and chatter that surrounded him, he turned in the direction he now knew where to find her. He remained quiet and apart from the conversation, his attention returning frequently to the table of six.

Sometime later, her group stood to depart, and he watched as Sarona and Thomas moved in the direction of the elevators. His stomach twisted with agitation as he tried to ignore the pictures his mind painted of the two, once they were beyond sight and behind closed doors.

*

Thomas insisted on seeing Sarona to her door, and though she would have preferred to say good-bye in the bar, she didn't want to appear rude. They said good night to the others at the elevators. Though Thomas was a handsome man with a gorgeous body, as far as she was concerned he needed a few lessons in manners and behavior. No matter how often she'd tried throughout the evening to distance herself, he never got the message. His roaming hands had gotten on her nerves and had almost ruined the entire evening. She was glad when everyone agreed it was time to go, sighting the next day's early morning class as reason enough to call it a night. She was tired. She'd had a long hard day playing at escape and evasion, she laughingly thought—avoiding David all day and swatting at Thomas all night. She'd had enough.

"Good night, Thomas. Thank you for walking me to my door. I guess I'll see you tomorrow," Sarona said brightly as she reached out to shake his hand.

"Yeah, sure, but the night doesn't have to end just yet, does it?" Thomas asked in a husky voice as he moved forward and grasped Sarona's arms, pulling her in close and tight against his body. His rock-hard arousal was full and apparent as he held her firmly against him. The unexpected move took her completely by surprise, leaving her shocked and speechless. Unfortunately, Thomas mistook her silence as agreement and proceeded to clamp his mouth down upon hers and delivered, at least in his mind, what had to be the most sensuous mind-blowing kiss a woman could experience.

Sarona was stunned, stiff and unresponsive. Thomas slowly released his grip. Letting his tongue and lips trail along her neck, he whispered in her ear, "Relax baby. Just let it happen naturally. I'm going to make it good for you, I promise."

Still in shock, Sarona slowly and carefully extricated herself from his arms and stepped back. "Uh, thanks for the offer, Thomas, but um, I'm not interested in taking this night any farther. I don't know where you got that impression, but I'm not attracted to you, nor am I interested in having sex with you."

"Come on, Sarona, you know you want to," Thomas said with a knowing look and coaxing tone. "We're away from everybody else now; you don't have to pretend anymore that you don't want the same thing I do. You can drop the act now, and stop teasing and playing hard to get.

Sarona looked at the man like he had two heads growing out of his neck. A flash of fury lit her eyes and added a rosy flush of color to her face. "Excuse me? Pretending, teasing, and playing hard to get? At what point in the evening did I give you the impression that I *wanted* your monkey grabbing hands all over me?"

She was angry—so angry she had to make a conscious effort to keep her voice even. She placed one hand on her hip and started waving the finger of her other hand in his face and under his nose.

"Listen up, lover boy. I don't know how you got this far in life thinking you're an expert on reading signs and signals, but I assure you, you need to take a refresher course in body language interpretation. Specifically, a woman's body language. I suggest you go back to school and take several notes on the subject. I also suggest that before you act on what you *think* you know; maybe you'd better *ask* somebody. Now, I'll chalk up your error in judgment to a simple case of downright ignorance, and I'll overlook your Neanderthal-like behavior this time, but any such *errors* in the future will not be tolerated. Do I make myself clear?"

Thomas was obviously taken aback by her vehement reaction and the fury on his face showed it. He made an aggressive, intimidating move toward Sarona, having every intention of responding with a few choice words of his own. Unfortunately, his response was preceded by reaching out to grab her arm, which proved to be another error in judgment. Sarona, automatically pre-empting a perceived attack, grabbed his arm, twisted it inward, and brought it up with a hard jerk, while simultaneously pressing hard into the pressure point located on his hand, at the base of his middle finger. The move had Thomas on his knees and in excruciating pain from his wrist to his shoulder in two seconds flat.

"Damn, Sarona, I'm sorry, I'm sorry!" Thomas screeched in pain. "What the fuck? All you had to do was say no!"

Sarona leaned over and spoke directly into his ear. "This *is* how I say no to idiots who don't know how to take *no* for an answer. You're damned lucky I didn't grab your balls and rip them out through your pant leg. Maybe I will, next time. But, there won't be a next time, will there?"

"No! No! *Hell* no!"

"As I said before," Sarona said sweetly as she slowly released his hand to allow him to rise to his feet, "good night, Thomas."

Thomas got to his feet and warily backed away. Holding his injured arm protectively against his body, he quickly turned and rushed away down the hall, not once looking back. He couldn't get down the hall and disappear fast enough, but not before she heard him muttering something under his breath about a "crazy-ass bitch."

Sarona entered her suite, chuckling to herself at the sight of Thomas scurrying down the hall. It was too bad she had to rough up her *date*—she laughed out loud as she made a few ninja-like moves and a couple karate chops in the air at an invisible foe—but he had it coming. It looked as though those lessons in self-defense had finally paid off. It wasn't her fault, really. It had been an automatic reaction she hadn't even realized her training had ingrained in her. It was the first time she'd felt threatened since taking the classes.

She sighed as she continued into the bedroom. She suspected that by tomorrow, if word got out that Thomas had bombed at the door, *his* account would probably be that she was either a lesbian or frigid. He'd probably defend his manhood by saying she didn't know what to do with a real man when he was standing right in front of her.

"It's too bad he doesn't have the first clue about how to behave like a 'real' man," Sarona muttered to herself. And that was the last thought she had on the matter of Mr. Thomas Khan.

*

David opened his eyes to the ringing of the phone, knowing without looking at the clock it was his morning wake-up call. He'd had another sleepless night; this time it had been spent lying awake tormented with the vision of Sarona and her date as they left the bar. His vivid imagination had held him hostage most of the night, making the morning courtesy call unnecessary.

He'd tossed and turned with the knowledge of what Thomas had in mind when he'd left with Sarona. He was a man and Sarona was a beautiful and enticing woman. David knew that, given the opportunity, he would do the exact same thing.

He'd stayed at the bar long enough to see Sarona and her group leave, and over the protests of Shelia and her friends he'd said good night and left as well. As tempted as he was to do so, he didn't follow them, but went straight to his room instead. He'd lain in tortured semi-slumber throughout the entire night, until now.

Tired and irritated from his lack of sleep, he hazarded a glance at the clock by the bedside. The illumination of the digital numbers indicated that he needed to be getting out of bed…now. It didn't matter that he'd had a crappy night; he had a full day ahead. Somehow, he had to strike a balance between his obligations and responsibilities to his firm and the reason for the trip, as well as fulfilling his need to accomplish his own personal goal, to get what he'd really come for.

What he'd come for was a chance at a fantasy and to realize a dream; to dive into the taste of delicious, creamy, sweet caramel. What he'd come for was an opportunity to get Sarona alone, and to tempt fate by stepping out onto a bridge constructed of desperate hope, to turn months of fantasies and dreams into reality. He hardened instantly at the random parade of thoughts in his head that all too often preceded an inevitable and ever-present want and desire.

He pushed the sheet away from his fully nude body in frustration, and the exposure to the cool air intensified the sensations of want and need. David slowly stretched to his full length and, gazing upon his lower half, he contracted the muscle in his penis that caused it to slowly rise and pulsate at half mast, while his balls tightened and withdrew inside his body. He closed his eyes and became wrapped in the vision of her totally nude and straddling his body, poised to lower herself down upon his erection. The image was more than he could stand. The ache in his balls was so sudden and sharp he had to grab himself to ease the intense pain brought on by such a graphic visual.

Breathing and easing himself through the pain, he was again reminded, albeit cruelly so, of how quickly time was running out. He slowly released the pressure on his groin and allowed his semi-erect shaft to slowly collapse into its normal state of rest. As painful as the feeling had been, there was still some pleasure in the thought of anticipation. Sighing in resignation, David threw the sheet completely back and prepared to face the unavoidable; another day of being so close to a dream that was still so far out of reach.

Chapter 5

Wednesday

Wednesday proved to be an experience in déjà vu. Sarona had again successfully hedged and dodged her way around all his attempts to make contact or conversation.

During an afternoon break, he stood away from the crowd, indulging in a solitary moment of brooding. He was mulling over his problem when he caught a glimpse of Thomas, who appeared distant and standoffish from the rest of his colleagues. Judging by his behavior and reluctance at being near Sarona, David guessed the evening hadn't turned out quite the way he'd hoped. The tell-tale signs of his evident failure brought a sense of momentary relief from his own anguish and frustration, and a grim smile to his face. On the one hand, it was reassuring to see Sarona was still in rare form, shooting down every advance as efficiently as a military commander in battle directing his troops and covering his flank. And he was glad to know he wasn't the only one who'd been shot down in action.

On the other hand…well, on the other hand it was annoyingly frustrating to be lumped into the same category as the likes of Thomas and Bruce. At the risk of letting pride and arrogance rule good sense, he'd like to think he'd impressed her more than the average Joe; that he stood out and had a lot more in his favor than the few who were currently passing for competition.

He was annoyed she was being difficult. While he had surely known on some level this would be an undertaking of considerable challenge, it never occurred to him how tough the challenge would be. Obviously, he'd underestimated the woman.

He'd relied too heavily on using his charm and good looks to influence her. In addition to his natural scent, they were his best assets, and he wasn't being given the chance to employ them. As he watched her head back to her class, David's lips tightened with abrupt resolve. He made up his mind then and there he would no longer be summarily dismissed. If she didn't want his company, fine. But she would no longer be allowed to avoid him at every turn; she was going to have to tell him, face-to-face. He knew a thing or two about planning strategies as well. He would re-evaluate his methods and come up with an alternate plan. He was going to have to take her completely by surprise and make a full-out frontal assault when she was most vulnerable, and when she least expected it.

He looked across the crowded restaurant and saw Sarona seated alone at a table for two, and he was next in line when the hostess returned from seating the previous patron. Seeing a golden opportunity, he beamed brightly, turned on the charm, and asked to be seated with the lady at the table in the back.

David smiled in anticipation as the hostess brought him to Sarona's table.

She sighed when she saw him and muttered, just loud enough for him to hear, "I knew I should have ordered in."

The hostess said, "This gentleman would like to join you for dinner. Is that all right?"

"Yes, of course, I'd be delighted. Hello, David."

Delighted, my ass, he thought with a silent smirk. He wasn't the least bit fooled. The look of annoyance in her eyes clearly contradicted the smile pasted on her lips. Well, too damn bad. She was stuck with him for now.

"Hi, Sarona. I'm not intruding, am I?" He was merely being polite in the asking; intruding or not, he didn't really give a damn.

"No, of course not. It'll be nice to have company," she answered in her most cheerful voice...and nearly choked on the lie as it crossed her lips.

David graciously thanked the hostess and pulled out his chair to seat himself. Sarona had responded a bit too cheerfully in his opinion. He put his arms on the table and, folding his hands together, gave her a long, accusing look. She hastily lowered her eyes to shield herself from his reproachful gaze, exhibiting a sudden intense interest in the menu. Realizing she wasn't going to react to his accusatory posture, David took up his own menu to browse.

The waitress brought bread and butter and returned with their choice of drinks. Eventually they both chose entrees and waited for their orders to arrive. The two passed the meal in polite conversation, and though it wasn't all bad, there was a palpable difference between the tone of tonight's dialogue and that of only two nights ago. There was neither teasing nor joking, nor the back-and-forth bantering he'd come to crave. *It's as though we're starting all over again*, he thought in frustration.

They continued through dessert in much the same manner until David, unable to endure the subdued tenor any longer, decided enough was enough.

"I'm not going to let you do it, you know," he said, staring into her eyes with a hard, steely look, idly circling the rim of his glass with his fingers.

"Do what?" Sarona asked with eyebrows drawn and a confused look on her face.

"Ignore me."

"Ignore you?"

"Yes, ignore me, and I think you go out of your way to do it too," he responded with mild irritation.

"I have no idea what you're talking about."

"Sure you do. You've avoided me for the past two days. Every time you saw me headed your way, you beat feet in the opposite direction, making sure our paths never crossed. You escaped and evaded at every turn like some kind of military Special Operations expert. You were damn good at it too. Hell, Sarona, you make me feel like I'm some kind of disease you don't want to catch. The time I've managed to spend with you is because I've pushed myself on you—forced you to acknowledge me. As a matter of fact, if I hadn't cornered you here at dinner, I have no doubt that if you'd seen me coming you would have disappeared long before now. The only reason I'm here is because you're too polite to say no, even though I've intruded and invited myself to share your dinner table. That's what I like about you, Sarona," David continued in a low quiet voice. "Even though you go out of your way to avoid me, you aren't actually rude about it. Tell me, what have I done to make you dislike me so?"

*

Sarona was shocked. She had no idea that, one, her avoidance of him had been so obvious, and two, that it bothered him. She couldn't believe he would take notice of such a thing in the first place. "I don't dislike you, David. I can't imagine why you would think that, but if I've given you that impression, then I'm truly sorry."

"Then what is it, Sarona? Why do you run every time you see me coming?"

She hated to admit it but the man had her pegged. Somehow he'd seen past her attempts to elude him and had totally misinterpreted her intention in the process. Obviously she hadn't been as successful as she'd thought, and had relayed the wrong message entirely. She didn't dislike him. God knows he couldn't be further from the truth. And now that she'd been confronted, his question had caught her completely off guard. As much as she didn't want to give him a reason to continue his pursuit, she knew she couldn't allow his misinterpretation to remain between them.

After considering her options she finally took a deep breath and, looking him straight in the eye, replied in a clear and defiant voice, "Self-preservation."

David returned her straightforward look, and broke out into a broad grin. "Please explain."

Not impressed by his teasing manner or wanting to waste time with pretenses, Sarona sighed in resignation. In need of fortification she took a sizeable sip of wine and answered, "David Broussard, you are one lethal and dangerous man. You're handsome, charming, witty, and you know exactly what to say to get and hold a woman's attention. You exude sexuality and wield the power to make women lose their minds and deliver all control into your hands. I'll be honest and admit that I'm not unaffected by your looks and charm, but I absolutely refuse to relinquish my control to a man who has little to no regard for the aftermath or consequences of his reckless use of such power—a man who goes through women like a cold through Kleenex. Though I also find you as witty and charming as every other woman on the face of this earth does, I have no desire to be a part of your entourage, or to become a member of the David Broussard fan club."

He leaned back in his chair, as if stunned by the magnitude of this revelation, and seemed hard pressed for an immediate response.

She was shocked at what she'd told him. She'd had no idea the things she'd said would come out of her mouth, but it was out there now, and there was no taking it back. She watched an array of expressions play across his face as he processed her uncensored response. When she saw the hard glint in his eyes and a sly smile she immediately distrusted slowly spread across his lips, she knew at once she'd made a mistake. She had unintentionally baited the tiger.

After a moment, David said, "I need to change your opinion of me, Sarona. I'm hardly the heartless destroyer of feminine virtue you accuse me of being. And not all these women I'm supposed to have deceived and misled belong inside that picture of innocence you paint. Yes, I'll admit I browse the market, and I do sample the wares from time to time, but in my defense, I'm simply responding to the expectations of every woman and man here. I'm already prejudged for my so-called roguish good looks, and because of this there is a certain level of anticipation. Everyone, men and women alike, expect me to play the ladies' man. If you ask me, *I'm* the victim here—the victim of exploitation. Basically, I'm being used to fulfill the longings and fantasies of others too inhibited or too afraid to do it for themselves."

"You can save your little 'woe is me' act, David, I'm not buying it. Living up to others' expectations is a choice, not a requirement. It looks to me like this role of martyrdom you've taken on is self-appointed. And I can't help but notice that, for all your complaining, you don't seem to be too put out by this part you play. So, why are you here, David?" she asked, aggravation clearly apparent in her voice. "Why do you persist in inviting yourself into my space and forcing me to acknowledge you? What do you want? Are you suddenly interested in sampling my wares too?" she snapped sarcastically.

David leaned forward. His face inches from hers and staring directly into her eyes, he said in an intimately suggestive voice,

"No, Sarona, I know a sample would never be enough. Once I get a taste of you, I know I'm going to want it all."

She felt the heat rise from the base of her neck, spread up her throat, and plaster itself all over her face and ears. Her face was on fire. She'd actually blushed! Finding herself once again suddenly at a loss for words and too flustered to remain, there was no other choice but to leave or be caught up and burned alive by his seductive powers.

Sarona rose from her seat, and in a voice that sounded more in control than she actually felt, she said, "I'm a firm believer in evolution's theories of survival of the fittest and self-preservation. You trigger my fight or flight response, and I admit, though cowardly it may be, quite frankly, I choose to flee. I think this would be a good point at which to say good night. Good night, David."

Sarona picked up her bill and left him sitting alone at the table with an unreadable expression upon his face.

*

He watched her walk away, watched her hips sway from side to side to a rhythm he couldn't hear but one he surely felt, the beat of it thrumming its way through his entire body, in perfect sync with that sway. He was hard and hurting with his desire for her, and his expression was an exact reflection of his physical state, set and hard as stone. She couldn't know it, but she'd fired his drive, fueled his resolve, and intensified his already unbearable obsession.

"I guess we'll have to find a way to deal with that trigger, won't we, Sarona?" David whispered to himself as he lifted his glass in a silent salute to her retreating backside. Although Sarona's backside was enticing to watch as she disappeared from sight, the repeating scenario was becoming an irritating routine. She'd already managed to avoid him for two days, so there was no way he was going to let her get away from him now.

If she thought she would be allowed to just walk away and consider that the end of story then she didn't know him as well as she thought she did. In fact, she didn't really know him at all. It was time he introduced his real self to the lady, David thought as he turned his drink bottoms up and drained the glass. Setting the empty glass down, he stood to go after Sarona with one thought on his mind—there was no time like the present.

*

She knew she'd made a mistake. He'd gotten to her, had slipped past that nonchalant exterior she had perfected, projected, and wrapped around herself like a shield. He had gotten a ringside look at what really went on beneath the surface of her feigned indifference, and she knew it was only a matter of time before he'd take advantage of his discovery.

Damn! She'd slipped up and she couldn't take it back. His showing up unexpectedly like that had taken her completely by surprise. She should have just said no; should have lied and said she was waiting for someone. Of course, the lie would have been obvious when no one showed up. And a man like David would have hung around to see if anyone did.

Sarona held her breath as she walked away, praying to God he wouldn't follow her and push to continue their discussion. But, as she prepared to pay for her meal, a hand reached out and took her arm and the bill, and the voice attached to it said, "I wouldn't be much of a gentleman if I didn't take care of this and at least escort you to your room."

As much as she wanted to protest, good sense dictated that she not argue the point. She allowed David to pay her dinner bill and reluctantly waited for him to escort her to the elevator. They rode in silence, watching the floors flash by on the wall panel, each in their own, thought-filled world. When they reached her floor, David held the doors open and allowed her to exit first. He walked her to her suite and then held out his hand for her key card, still silent.

"Thank you, David, but this really isn't necessary." He remained standing there silently with his hand extended.

"Fine!" Exasperated, she handed him the card. He leaned over, inserted it into the slot, and pushed the door open.

As she accepted the return of her key, she felt she should make one last attempt at clearing the air between them. After all, she liked David. She just didn't want to be a part of whatever game he was playing. "Look, David, I apologize for my outburst. I'm sorry I was so abrupt, but I thought I should clear up any misconceptions you might have about you and me. I know where you think this is going but I can assure you, as far as I'm concerned, it goes no farther than right here, right now."

He ignored her apology and protest and leaned forward. In a silky voice, low and husky, he asked, "What are you afraid of, Sarona? What do you think could happen between us? And what if something did happen; would that be such a bad thing? If you'd lighten up and let yourself go to explore the possibilities, you might be surprised. You just might enjoy it."

Staring into his incredibly sexy brown eyes, Sarona felt a loss of control, vulnerable and cornered with her back against the wall. She was infuriated with the feeling. Her anger was in her voice, captured in her stance and seen in eyes that glittered with belligerent defiance.

"I don't understand why you're here and insisting on wasting your time and mine. We both know I'm not your type, that I'm not what you want; your history with women speaks to that. I've seen the kind of woman who gets your attention and I'm smart enough to know I don't fit into that mold."

He leaned in closer to her, his face a scant few inches from hers, never touching. He let his nose follow the contour of her shoulder, the curve of her neck, the fragrance of her hair, inhaling deeply, as if drawing in and savoring the smell of her.

She felt it. He felt it. The pull of an electrical undercurrent between them so strong she was certain they would ignite, explode, and burst into flames right then and there. It was the most erotic thing she had ever experienced, and it left her breathless, dizzy, and swaying, waiting for the air to return to her lungs. She stood stark still as he pulled back to stare straight into her eyes. Her eyes looked at his lips, mesmerized by his masculine beauty; her ears were captivated by the seductive whisper of a uniquely unsettling voice, calm and unhurried, filled with intense yet controlled emotion—a voice dangerously close to making her lose all sense of direction, place, and time.

"Those other women you allude to were merely a passing interest, a phase in my life when the appearance of the container meant more than its content. Meeting you, being with you, has shown me a whole new meaning to the phrase 'you can't judge a book by its cover.' I like the cover your book comes wrapped in, and I look forward to exploring it, page by page, from cover to cover. I won't be satisfied until your pages are thumbed and worn from use, and every word and phrase is committed to memory." He continued to stare into her liquid brown eyes, determined to make his intentions known and understood.

"The only misconceptions here, Sarona, are the ones you have fixed in your mind. I'm telling you right here, right now that no matter what you may think you know, you don't know who I am, and you have no idea what I want *or* what I desire. But I intend to inform you in no uncertain terms."

He reached out his hand and, with two extended fingers, lifted her chin. Though her mind rebelled, her lips trembled with anticipation, waiting for the brush of soft, tender flesh on flesh. "You know what your problem is, Sarona?" he asked in a husky whisper, the sound of his voice echoing down her spine as the pad of his thumb brushed back and forth and stroked the fullness of her bottom lip. "You think too much." His eyes held her captivated as he lowered his head. He took her mouth with his own—claimed, captured, and took possession and enveloped her in a fire so hot and so intense, she was certain she'd burn up and turn into ashes right there where she stood.

The kiss, surprisingly light and tender, sent shock waves of warmth cascading throughout her body. His tongue licked her lips, separated and gently delved within, seeking out and caressing the recesses of her mouth. Her response was automatic as her mouth opened and melded to his.

Tongues touched, tasted, intertwined, and dueled for dominance, acceptance...liberation. The sensation was hot, sending nearly unbearable heat like liquid fire coursing through her veins, through her stomach, moving lower to pool at the juncture between her legs. Her nipples tightened, peaked, and protruded, suddenly sensitive to the brush of material stretched taut across her fully extended and aching breasts.

The feeling was electrifying, so profound she felt the heat generate a gush of moisture that thoroughly saturated and soaked her meager slip of underwear. Her mind melted, her body swayed, and her legs nearly buckled from the onslaught of sensations that flowed through and ravaged her entire body.

David reluctantly ended the kiss and released her chin then stepped back and pushed the door open for her to enter her suite. As she backed her way inside on less than stable footing, she heard him say in a voice filled with smug satisfaction, "I like kissing you, Sarona. It's definitely something we're going to have to do a lot more of, and much more often." He then turned and sauntered away, back down the hallway, and didn't look back.

*

"Hello?" came the sleep-laden sound of Joyce's voice on the other end of the telephone line.

"Joyce, I'm sorry, did I wake you?" Sarona asked. "I forgot about the time difference between here and there."

"Yeah, girlfriend," Joyce said, stifling a yawn, "but you know it's okay. What's up?"

"Joyce, I'm in trouble and I don't know what to do!" Sarona said, the tone of forlorn frustration evident in her voice. Joyce immediately came fully awake, alerted to the sound of her voice.

"What's wrong, what's happened?"

"I'm sorry; I don't mean to upset you. It's nothing life-threatening or serious, but it scares me, and I need you to tell me what to do!" Sarona wailed.

"Okay, okay. Just calm down and tell me what the problem is."

"It's David!"

"David?"

"Yes, David!" she nearly shouted.

"Sarona, darling, I'm confused. Who is David and what is the problem with him?"

"You know who David is. I told you about him, remember? Casanova?"

"Casanova?" Joyce repeated, still clueless about where the conversation was leading.

"Yes!"

"Sarona, sweetheart, it's one in the morning here. You need to refresh my memory if you expect me to know who or what you're talking about."

"Okay, right," Sarona said. "I'll start from the beginning. Remember when I told you about how lately, it seemed everywhere I traveled there was this white guy who was just so fine, smelled so good, and had all the women running after him, and how he always seemed to pop up in my face wanting to talk?"

"Yeah, I do remember something like that. You said he looked like a Greek God and that he gave off some kind of natural pheromones that drove women wild."

"That's right, that's him, that's David!"

"I take it David's there with you on this trip as well?"

"Uh huh."

"Something happened?"

"Well, yes…no…uh, not yet."

"Okay, sweetie, it's too late in the night to play twenty questions. Why don't you just tell me what happened."

Sarona sat back and, propping herself up on the bed pillows, she began to recount her encounters with David over the past thirty-six hours. She left nothing out, describing how he had engineered their initial meeting, how great the conversation had been, how she had come to the realization he was interested in more than just conversation, that he had confronted her and told her he didn't like the way she treated him, and finally how he had, more or less, issued an edict, punctuated with that mind-blowing kiss, not forgetting to include how she was affected and how her body had reacted to said kiss.

"It was the hottest, most erotic, mind-numbing experience I've ever had in my entire life! My lips are still trembling, my body is still shaking, and my underwear is drenched! I'm sitting here waiting for my heart to stop pounding!"

"Well, it sounds to me like you've had an interesting few days," Joyce said with a chuckle. "So tell me, my dear, because I feel I'm missing something here, what's the problem? He's handsome, intelligent, and imaginative, has a great personality, and it sounds like he's pretty smart because he's attracted to you. All this sounds like pretty positive things in his favor to me. And, since I know you so very well, I know the problem can't be because he's white."

"No, of course it isn't. I don't care about that. The problem is he's such a player! He has women trailing and chasing after him everywhere we go, and I don't want to be one of them."

"I'm confused, Sarona. You say the women chase after him. How does that make him a player?"

"Well, he doesn't try to discourage them or send them away. And since I've known him, I've never seen the man with the same woman twice. If you ask me, it's like he's working on a Guinness World Record of how many women one man can sleep with in his lifetime."

"Honey, he's a man! You can't expect him or any red blooded, full-grown man to turn away feminine advances. You're a woman; you know how determined and ruthless we can be when we want something. Contrary to popular belief that men are the stronger sex, I don't think there's a man alive who can withstand the will of a woman when she has her mind made up. And, when it comes to a woman offering sex, why would he want to?

"Girl, you know this all started with Adam and Eve and that apple." Joyce suddenly lowered her voice to a hushed tone as though imparting some dark secret. "If Adam had had any sense or willpower, he would have just said no, but you *know* she came at him waving more than that apple in his face! And thus," she stated with over-exaggerated significance, "the 'weakness' was born, giving every man alive a biblical excuse to justify his inability to resist a woman's wiles. 'The devil made me do it' has become the mantra of millions."

"Stop it!" Sarona bubbled with laugher. "Don't you dare blame this on Eve!"

"I'm serious! Eve was the mother of more than the human race, she was the mother of *working it*...and women have been waving and working it ever since! I'm not lying. Check the history books! There are Marc Antony and Cleopatra, Samson and Delilah, and Bill Clinton and Monica Lewinsky."

"You know, Joyce—" She chuckled at her friend's outrageous rationalization. "—in some twisted way, with your twisted logic, sometimes you actually make sense."

"I know," Joyce replied with smug satisfaction. "I have some questions for you," she added, returning to the sincerity of Sarona's concern. "Is he married?"

"No."

"Is he engaged?"

"No, I don't think so."

"Is he obligated in any way to some other woman?"

"No, not that I know of. Actually, he seems to be between relationships," Sarona murmured, remembering Shelia Preston.

"Okay, so far so good. Do you like him?"

"Yes."

"Do you find him physically attractive?"

"Oh, God, yes!" Sarona gushed as memory fluttered through her body, reminding her precisely how deep the attraction went.

"Then I don't see a problem here, Sarona. If you're both attracted to one another, there are no other outside complications, and you're both consenting adults, then I say let go and let nature take its course."

"But what about all those other women?"

"What about them? Do you know if any of what you've seen has any basis in fact, or are you simply letting your eyes determine what your mind believes? How many times have you been lied about or gossiped about because of something someone *thought* they saw? Don't penalize him for being a man, Sarona, and don't let things you have no control over control you."

"But Joyce, a man like David can wreak havoc on a woman's ability to reason! In only two short nights, he's worked his charm and managed to make me feel special, desired, and almost... important. I admit I like how he makes me feel right now, but I also admit that I'm a coward; I don't want to deal with the aftermath when it's done and over and he moves on."

"I understand the need to feel special and desired, Sarona. I think we all, as women, have that embedded in our DNA. We are, after all, the more romantic of our species. And I know you have your reasons for holding back, but girl, if it was me—and you know me—I would catch the wave, go with the flow, and enjoy the ride. Why waste time worrying about how it's going to end before it even begins? If it ends, it ends. But, for this moment, if you feel special, desired and almost important, then embrace the feeling. It may never come again, or maybe it might never end. Life is about chances, Sarona. Take a chance."

"I know I'm blowing this all out of proportion, but I'm scared, Joyce. I'm scared of what this could turn into...scared of what he could do to me."

"Don't get me wrong. I know your concerns are valid, and I'm not saying to totally throw caution to the wind, Sarona. It's okay to be scared; fear can be a good thing, most of the time. It's there for a reason, to protect us; but sometimes if we think too hard and too long, it can be a hindrance that disables and cheats us out of the what-ifs in life. Don't let it do that to you, girlfriend. Don't let it hinder your heart, deny your desires, or take away the moments that can take your breath away."

"I hear what you're saying, Joyce," Sarona said with a sigh of acceptance. "I guess I needed to hear it come from someone else, someone I trust. It's why I always call you. You're the voice of reason to the crazy chaos that goes on in my head sometimes. I'm sorry I woke you, but I'm glad you're there. Thanks for listening."

"It's not a problem. That's what I'm here for."

"Besides," Joyce said with an unmistakably mischievous lilt to her voice, "need I remind you of just how long it's been since you've had sex? I mean, shout hallelujah, reaching for the rafters, no holds barred sex with another living, breathing human being, and *not* the battery operated kind."

"No, you do not!" Sarona laughingly responded. A vivid memory of her detailed fantasy flashed through her mind, and suddenly she was a little embarrassed at just how close to the truth her friend really was.

*

She needed a stiff drink, and the bourbon she found stocked in the suite bar would do just fine. As she swallowed the sparkling amber liquid, she prayed it would somehow magically erase the taste of his kiss and eradicate the memory of his electrifying touch. The feel of his lips had been warm, soft, and silky; the taste of his breath hot and sweet in her mouth—a perfect melding and mingling of moist heat and flavor together. His alluring scent still lingered in her nose, and the look of pure, carnal hunger that burned in his eyes haunted her mind—a hunger she was certain had been mirrored in her own.

She wondered at the intensity of the fire that burned him from within; the depth of his passion, the height of his desire. And she feared he would stop at nothing to assuage his need to satisfy both. His touch had set her on fire, and his kiss had left her in a state of arousal and anticipation. The combination of the two had her balancing precariously on the border between good common sense and sheer insanity.

She reluctantly acknowledged that David's declaration had been a turning point for the both of them. He'd made it clear what he wanted, and he wanted her. That one kiss had brought about a change—a change that provided perfect clarity. She now saw clearly what she'd feared the most—the inevitable. She knew with reluctant conviction she was destined to take the next step and drop her defenses, ignore her reservations, and give in to her yearning.

She reached up and lightly brushed trembling fingertips across lips that still tingled from a kiss that burned in her mind and was imprinted on her soul. Emitting an inward sigh of defeat, she closed her eyes and made one last acknowledgement: she was in danger of losing her tenuous grip on common sense and giving up her soul to say yes to the devil himself. Tonight's turning point had swiftly become a point of no return.

Chapter 6

David had not escaped unscathed. For all his show of control as he'd sauntered down the hall, his legs were as unsure and shaky as a newborn colt. He ignored the fact that his heart beat at a runaway pace and his groin was full to the point of bursting, his shaft rock hard and aching.

Once inside the elevator, his pretense of calm and control dissolved completely. He pushed the button to his floor and leaned forward, resting his head against the panel, struggling for composure. If one stolen pleasure could evoke such a potent and powerful response, then God help him when they took it to the next level!

Once inside his room, he was too keyed up to relax. His senses were too raw and sensitive from the sensations that seared him from the inside out. Residual warmth from the heat of that one kiss flowed along his nerve endings. He was rocked by the feel of her soft lips, the taste of her mouth, the fragrance of her hair, and the sweet scent of erotic musk that lingered on his skin and teased his senses. It was as though he had reached out and touched fire, drawn like a moth to its flame. He knew it and couldn't keep himself from it, because like the moth, he needed to tempt fate. He needed to tease the heat and flick his fingers back and forth through the blaze, to deny the danger and defy the inevitable—being scorched, seared, or burned alive by the tempered heat of the flame.

He had a sinking feeling he truly was playing with fire. Although he was painfully aware of Sarona's reluctance to move beyond more than conversation, he'd made clear his intentions and expectations. She couldn't say she hadn't been warned. And, although she may have been caught off guard by that unexpected kiss, her response was scorching hot and filled with passion; a passion he planned to explore further. He'd taken the next step and there was no turning back.

With too many thoughts in his head, plagued by his imagination and libido, he decided he needed to get out of the room and do something to take his mind off Sarona. Maybe a trip to the hotel gym would help to work off some nervous energy. Changing into gym attire and snatching up a towel and a bottle of water, he left in search of respite.

*

Shelia had decided to indulge herself with a late evening visit to the hotel pool. On her way to her room she passed the gym and glanced through the large window that served as an outer wall. She saw David on a treadmill, running hard in an all-out sprint, his body gleaming with perspiration, his muscles hard, taut, and tempting. His tall, golden-bronze frame, his wet, bouncing curls and long legs clad in form-fitting shorts spawned latent memories of sweaty sheets and tangled limbs, and she shuddered with memory at the sight of his body in fluid motion.

"Hi," she breathed in her sexiest voice. "It looks like you've been working hard; you're all…hot…and sweaty. Are you about done?" she asked, a hungry look in her eyes and pouty lips pursed in practiced perfection.

"Actually, yes, I am," David said as he reached to turn off the machine and began to towel himself dry. "What brings you here this time of night?"

"I was taking a late-night dip in the pool. Had I'd known you were here I would have asked you to join me. It might have been like old times, with the exception of swimsuits." Her throaty laughter filled the room as she alluded to times together spent skinny-dipping in his private pool after midnight. Still eyeing his body hungrily, she made a not-so-subtle move to stand in front of him and reached up to stroke his chest, letting her hand drift lower to pause at the waist of his running shorts.

"You do remember those midnight dips, don't you?" Her gaze scanned his face and body appreciatively, in search of an encouraging response.

She didn't bother concealing her obvious desire. She wanted him, and she wanted him to know and remember. David remembered those same midnight dips, acknowledged her look of lust, tolerated her touch…and felt nothing. He wasn't surprised. He hadn't felt anything for Shelia or any other woman from his past in months. His attention and attraction had been for one woman and one woman only.

"Yes, I remember," David responded with an icy smile, skillfully capturing her wrist and restraining her hand from exploring further. He took Shelia by the shoulders and put her off to one side so he could step back and pointedly place the treadmill between them. His actions were deliberate. He wanted her to understand that things were different now. He no longer had an interest in what was once between them. It was all in the past, and the past was where he wanted to leave it.

"What's going on, David?" Shelia's irritation was obvious. "Why do you persist in playing this game of yours? Why are you acting like you're no longer interested in being together?"

"It's not a game, Shelia, and I'm not acting. I told you months ago the situation was no longer working for me. I lost interest. It happens. You need to accept it, let go, and move on."

"Accept it? I'm supposed to simply give up? You actually *expect* me to give up? You can do that—forget we were together? I don't understand, David. How can you act so cold, as though the time we spent together never happened, like we never existed?"

"I'm not denying we ever existed. It was fun while it lasted, but what we had was just sex, Shelia, nothing more. Either of us can find 'just sex' anywhere, with anyone. I've realized I want more out of a relationship than merely the sexual aspect. Sure, you and I had great sex, but we never had intimacy. I want a chance at having both, or, at least something more than what we had together or what I've experienced with every other woman I've been with."

She laughed at his revelation. "But sex is what you're good at, David," she purred. "Why complicate a perfectly good relationship with 'something more'?" He refused to respond and merely continued to give her a cold stare.

"God, David, you sound like a woman!" she snapped, annoyed that he was unresponsive. "And where do you expect to find 'more'?" She sneered. "Certainly not with Sarona Maxwell."

"Whatever I do, and whomever I do it with, is none of your business, is it?" David replied, irritated with her doggedly persistent interrogation and annoyed she'd brought Sarona into the conversation.

"Don't be silly. Of course it's my business!" she snapped. "I hope you don't think I'm going to just step aside simply because you think you've had some sort of revelation. We're two of a kind David, you and me. We're superficial and shallow people, uninterested in depth or dimension. We belong together."

"What do you want, Shelia?" he asked, quiet anger underlying his question.

"I want us to pick up where we left off, or start over, at whatever point you want, I don't care. Let's just end this ridiculous standoff and get back together."

"That's not going to happen. I told you, I'm not interested."

"You're not interested?" she repeated, her voice rising distinctively. "I've got news for you. I don't know who you think you're dealing with, but I'm nothing like those other women you've played with, or used and dropped! I won't be put on the curb like yesterday's garbage, and I *won't* be ignored!"

Shelia was nearly shouting, her voice on the verge of hysteria. She abruptly turned on her heel and walked away, her face flaming red and her back ramrod stiff.

David watched her stalk off, painfully aware of the anger radiating off her body in waves. He was relieved she'd left, but he knew this wouldn't be the end of it. He had an uneasy feeling he'd be seeing her again, and he knew it would bode nothing but trouble when he did. Dreading the prospect of another unwanted confrontation, David gathered up his towel and water bottle and left, his quest for solitude ruined by Shelia's unexpected appearance and tantrum.

*

Thursday
His initial sense that time was of the essence was reinforced by the knowledge it was passing much too quickly. And with a mere two days left, his sense of urgency was more pressing than ever. Right now, he was worried. He didn't know what to expect after his stunt from the night before. He'd spent the entire night tossing and turning, praying he hadn't blown his chances. He counted on the fact that she hadn't slapped him silly as a good sign, or at the very least encouraging.

He'd intended the kiss to be light and subtle, an open invitation and enticement to explore and experience more of what he could offer. But his plan might have backfired. Much like playing a game of chess, he'd taken a calculated risk. He replayed last night's kiss over and over in his head, reliving the powerful sensations of desire and need that had coursed through his body and left behind the feeling of molten heat. His mind was stuck in perpetual rewind, captivated by the memory of her soft full lips, her mouth open and inviting, and her response—white-hot. If he were asked, he'd swear he'd felt his blood boil.

Her fragrant smell of sweet, spicy musk was embedded deeply and lingered in his nose. That one, brief kiss stirred his senses and set his body on fire, and had left him with a hard-on the size of Texas—a hard-on that had lasted all night and was still achingly evident today. Even now, though he knew his system probably wouldn't survive the impact of seeing her again, he searched the room anyway, hoping for a glimpse.

It was the midmorning break before lunch, and he had taken up position in what had become his customary observation point, once again using the hotel décor to hide himself from view. His eyes were dark, brooding, and inscrutable as he located Sarona and watched her from across the room. Like a tiger, he was a predator studying and stalking his prey. He was acutely aware he had only two nights to get Sarona in his arms and into his bed and to realize his dream fantasy of the past six months. His agitation brought to mind the sudden visual of the giant hourglass from *The Wizard of Oz,* a vivid reminder of how little time he had left. After last night's kiss, his desire and determination had kicked into overdrive.

*

She knew he was somewhere in the crowd watching her. She didn't know where, but she'd swear she could feel his eyes on her. She told herself she was being ridiculous, that no matter what Joyce had said and no matter what conclusions she'd come to in the middle of the night, she needed to keep her head on straight and forget about David Broussard.

This whole thing was insane! The man spelled bad trouble with a capital 'B.' Yet, no matter how hard she tried, she couldn't suppress the sensation evoked by the memory of his kiss, or the thrill of feeling wanted and desired. And he did want her; he made no secret of it. She knew that even though he was sexually attracted to her, it could all be just a game to him, but unfortunately for her, game or no game, she wasn't beyond feeling lightheaded at the prospect.

Rushing back toward her class, Sarona nearly had a heart attack as an arm snaked out from behind a large potted tree and grabbed her. A quick, firm pull forward had her chest-to-chest and face-to-face with familiar, laughing brown eyes. She was so taken by surprise, she forgot to register the outraged indignation she was sure she should have felt. Instead, she was immediately overcome with an electric pulse of anticipation, and she ignored the protest surging to her lips and allowed those amazing arms and beautiful eyes to pull her in and wrap her up in instant euphoria.

"What do you think you're doing, David?" she whispered as she pressed closer, her face automatically and expectantly turned upward, waiting for the delicious, silken touch of his lips, the taste of his mouth, and the demanding, unrelenting fire generated by his touch. She melted into him and let herself go liquid in his embrace.

"I'm stealing a kiss," he whispered back.

*

She was livid! Shelia nearly choked at the sight—the two of them embracing and kissing! They were obscured by one of the many potted trees located throughout the hallway but from her vantage point she was able to recognize them and witness the sickening sight for herself. It wasn't enough that he ignored her and made her beg for his attention, or that he embarrassed her in front of her friends. Now he publicly humiliated her with another woman! This was more than she would stand for. *Something has to be done*, she thought to herself as she turned and angrily stalked away.

*

David felt like a teenager back in high school, waiting for the final bell to ring. Waiting for the afternoon session to end was grueling. His mind was filled with all things Sarona, and he was impatient to get back to her.

He'd spent his afternoon reliving today's unexpected kiss and the unforgettable feeling of her body melded to his. He hadn't expected his immediate response to her when he saw her again. As she passed, his hand reached out as if with a mind of its own. She hadn't hesitated, hadn't pulled away. This kiss was more intimate and more exciting, stolen in secret, in hidden recesses away from prying eyes.

He took advantage of the unexpected, and while Sarona was caught off guard, he asked her out. He'd played dirty and pulled out all the stops. He'd resorted to out-and-out seduction to get her to agree, and he wasn't repentant. He was prepared to use every tactic in his bag of tricks, if he had to. Though he had to cajole, convince, and virtually beg, he had gotten her to agree to meet him for dinner. This was no minor victory. It was a triumph and an enormous step toward his ultimate goal: to get Sarona to surrender herself into his capable hands.

"Go out to dinner with me, Sarona," he'd whispered in her ear while his lips skimmed along her neck, brushed against her cheek and softly planted a string of kisses on her lips, from corner to corner. He'd cradled her in his arms and held her close to his chest while he whispered in her ear.

"Say yes, Sarona."

"What?" she'd stammered.

"Not what—yes. Say yes."

"I don't know, David. Maybe we should slow down—give ourselves a chance to catch our breath. Things are going a little too fast for me."

"I don't want to catch my breath, Sarona. I want to lose myself in the moment, in this moment. I want to stay right here, breathless, until I *have* to succumb to the need for air. In case you haven't noticed, we're on a very tight schedule. We don't have the luxury of time to indulge ourselves in safe and sane reactions. All we have is right here and right now, to do whatever we want. There isn't any time to waste on indecision and uncertainty. I know what I want. I want to spend whatever time I have left here with you. Tell me you don't want to do the same and I'll let it go, I won't pursue it any further…but I won't believe you." He'd looked into her eyes, the light of hope burning brightly. The amber color shimmered and glowed and beckoned her in, and she found herself falling and drowning in that limpid pool of primal desire.

"Say yes, Sarona," he'd whispered as his lips and teeth gently grazed and nibbled at her mouth. His heart beat so strongly she could feel the vibrations of it pulsating from his lips to hers. ". . . please…say yes."

*

Sarona was nervous about being alone with David. She was both appalled and thrilled by her reaction to him whenever he touched her. She blamed his combination of good looks, erotic smell, and charming personality for her loss of good common sense. Being with David was like walking through a minefield; it was a dangerous, explosive situation.

She'd tried to talk herself out of the date. She wanted to call and make some excuse, but nothing believable or plausible came to mind. There was nothing she could offer that would disguise her reason for other than what it truly was—cowardice. Sighing with resignation, she gathered her purse and wrap and left for the appointed place and time, her stomach knotted with excitement and trepidation.

*

Shelia sat at the bar, attempting to drown her anger in as many vodka martinis as the bartender could make and as fast as he could make them. She was desperately trying to erase the sight of David kissing Sarona from her mind. Unfortunately, the alcohol made the memory more vivid, more real.

It seemed as though time stopped while she'd stared in absolute horror at the scene that had played out in front of her. She'd stared in shock at the way he'd held her and at the look on his face as he'd pulled her close and kissed her. It was like looking at an old, black-and-white romance movie and watching the hero get the girl. She saw something on his face and in his eyes she'd never seen before, and it made her heart stop.

He looked…happy. This could not be happening! When she turned and stalked away, she'd been so furious she'd skipped her afternoon session altogether and went directly to her suite. She'd started drinking as soon as the door closed behind her, fueling her fury and rage to a dangerous point of eruption. Her mind was alternately consumed with feelings of denial and a plot for revenge.

She spent the entire afternoon trying to hatch a scheme to get back at David, but her thinking was too muddled by the alcohol to develop a clear plan of vengeance. Eventually, one possible solution finally managed to peek through. He had a reputation; everyone knew he was a player who thought nothing of using women for recreational sport. Maybe Sarona didn't know about his history. Maybe she was stupid enough to fall for his tricks, and it would serve her right if he used her and left her like he'd done with all the others. She refused to go away quietly, remanded to his list of discarded and forgotten conquests. It would be her pleasure to ruin his plans and expose his game.

Thoughts of retribution still ran high in her head as she sat at the bar waiting for the others to join her. Ellen and Linda were the first to arrive, and each took a seat on barstools next to Shelia. She listened with half an ear to the conversation that went on around her. Her mind was distracted as she scanned the lobby, hoping to see David. She would confront him and give him one last chance to come to his senses. If he didn't, then she would reveal her intentions to expose his notorious reputation to Sarona.

She was considering going to his room when she saw him standing near the hotel entrance, anxiously looking at his watch as though he were waiting for someone. He was obviously dressed for a date, and her anger flared again as she assumed he must be waiting for Sarona.

Her assumptions were confirmed when Sarona appeared, similarly dressed and moving in David's direction. Shelia was suddenly overcome with outrage, and the fire of jealousy and resentment streaked through her blood. With her eyes focused solely on Sarona and without conscious thought, she lurched off her barstool and moved forward with her mind hell bent on confrontation.

*

They had agreed to meet in the hotel lobby at six o'clock, then walk or catch a cab to one of the restaurants in the area. He'd done some checking and had decided on a quaint little Bistro, popular for its food, its wine, and its intimate atmosphere. He was anxious to spend more time with Sarona, and he wanted her all to himself, without outside interruptions or interference.

David watched her approach. She was gorgeous. Her hourglass figure, sultry eyes, delicious caramel colored complexion, and dazzling smile were all wrapped up in an amazing dress that showed just enough leg and cleavage to be sexy, alluring, and classy. The double-layer silk dress had a gathered waist, green print, and multicolor beaded detail. The fitted bodice emphasized her bust, flaring at the hips down to a hemline with a rippling effect around the knee. She wore open-toed sandals with three-inch heels, the color of sage with matching purse and shawl. He was again reminded of vintage Marilyn Monroe posters, and his cock came alive and stood at attention at the sight of her.

*

Sarona saw David waiting for her, so tall and so unbelievably handsome in a dark blue silk suit, an aqua blue shirt and a dark blue and black print tie, with a very large grin upon his face. *Damn, he looks good,* she thought as she moved toward him.

Just as she lifted her hand in greeting she was brought up short, startled by the sudden appearance of Shelia Preston directly in her path, her face marred and distorted in anger.

"I want to talk to you right now," Shelia hissed, her agitation blatantly apparent. "I know you've been sneaking around with David. I saw the two of you hiding behind bushes, kissing. And don't try to deny it," she snapped. "I can smell him all over you!"

"That's because he *was* all over me, not that it's any business of yours," Sarona stated calmly. "I don't understand your concern, Shelia. It's my understanding you and David are no longer involved. Not only has this been reported through the normal reliable gossip and grapevine resources, but I heard it from David himself."

Shelia's ranting had drawn the attention of patrons gathered in the lobby, and people began to stop and stare. Sarona wasn't exactly thrilled about the world witnessing her private involvement with David, but she wouldn't back down from a fight either. *Let the bitch rant,* she thought. *She'll make herself look exactly like the fool she is.*

"Do you think he's interested in you for more than sex?" Shelia seethed. "That's not how he operates. I've got news for you; you're just another notch in his bedpost! Every woman here knows the Broussard Method." Her voice rose to the verge of hysteria. "You're nothing more than an experiment. He's probably looking to experience a little jungle fever."

"Well, if, as you say, every woman here knows the Broussard Method, then every woman here except you knows when the deal is done and how to accept when it's time to move on. And as for his possible interest in jungle fever, my response to that would be—if a man like David feels he can achieve ultimate satisfaction by experimenting and stepping outside his normally tame parameters, all I can say is welcome to the jungle."

*

Momentarily stunned, David stopped in his tracks as he witnessed the spectacle that was Shelia. A moment later, he was galvanized into action to rush to Sarona's side, furiously protective and aggressive.

He reached the two women and was attempting to pull Shelia aside when Sarona placed her hand in his chest and said, "Back off, Broussard. This is between Shelia and me. She obviously has a lot on her mind, and I want to hear what it is."

David's arrival seemed to startle Shelia out of her single-minded rage. It was as though she had suddenly come to her senses and realized where she was—in the middle of an upscale hotel lobby, being stared at and making an absolute fool of herself. Suddenly, she was speechless.

"Are you done?" Sarona asked, exhibiting a cool and calm exterior that belied the fury within. When there was no response, Sarona shrugged her shoulders, turned, and walked away. In parting, she looked back over her shoulder and said, "You know, Shelia, I would think someone with your financial means would have invested in an education in manners or etiquette, since it's obvious you weren't taught either as a child." And, as if in afterthought, she added, "And if I were you, I'd be careful whose bedpost *your* notch appears on. It may save you from other embarrassments in the future."

David let Sarona move some distance ahead before he turned to Shelia and said in a lowered voice, rife with anger and disgust, "If you *ever* come near me or Sarona again, I'll have a restraining order issued against you in all fifty states!"

He left Shelia standing where she was as he hurried to catch up to Sarona. She was nearly at the lobby exit when he reached her.

The curious looks and murmurs of the crowd held no meaning for him. His mind and focus were on one thing only—getting to Sarona. He was aware of one thought—damage control. Would she still want to go out with him? Would she still want to be with him after such an exhibition?

The look in her eyes was unfathomable. He had no idea what she was thinking, but he was encouraged by the fact that she was still standing there waiting for him. Without a word, Sarona stretched out her hand, offering him her wrap, which he dutifully took and draped around her shoulders. Placing his hand at the small of her back and pushing the door open ahead of her, he escorted her from the hotel, taking them both from the further scrutiny of curious eyes.

David hailed a cab and gave the address of their destination. He then settled back and quietly held Sarona's hand, gently and tentatively stroking the soft smoothness he found clutched within his grasp. The trip was a short drive made in silence, each immersed within his or her world of thought.

*

They'd reached the restaurant in a matter of minutes, and were quickly seated and served drinks. The silence they'd shared inside the cab still lingered, and had now stretched beyond his point of tolerance. He was worried. Worried that Sarona would let Shelia's outrageous scene change or interfere with what was developing between them. He could have strangled Shelia with his bare hands! And, depending on the evening's outcome, he still might do it! For now, he was glad Sarona was still willing to have dinner with him. He didn't know if that was good or bad, but if need be, he was ready to defend himself, to plead his case.

She seemed distracted, deep in thought—of course, with good reason. The showdown with Shelia had to be uppermost in her mind. Unsure of how to proceed, he took a deep breath and decided to plunge right in. He reached across the table and took both her hands in his.

"I know what happened has probably caused you to second guess what's obviously developing with us, but please, Sarona, don't let what she did interfere and ruin something that could be so good between us."

Staring at how the flickering candlelight accented the contrast of their intertwined hands, David was captivated by the unexpected beauty of their colors mixed and mingled together.

"David, why do you think I would let anything Shelia said influence what or how I feel? Shelia is a bitter and vindictive woman, angry because she can no longer enjoy the status of being seen with you. She can't walk around and show you off as her prized possession anymore, and it burns her ass. Her wanting you back has nothing to do with sincere feelings. She simply misses being the talk and envy of every woman within a hundred mile radius. Don't worry—I don't blame you for Shelia's delusions of grandeur."

He was stunned by her comment and by her perfect perception of exactly who Shelia Preston was. Her statement said everything he himself had thought and felt—that to Shelia he was nothing more than a status symbol. A year ago, it wouldn't have mattered, because a year ago he was nearly as superficial and shallow as Shelia. It had taken nearly a year of abstinence and soul searching to help him discover he wanted something more out of life. And yes, as cliché as it may have sounded, he wanted something more meaningful. He had weighed and measured his life and found that he desperately needed to let go of his playboy persona to find what life had to offer beyond a superficial and shallow existence.

"So, are you saying you're willing to forget about Shelia's tirade?"

"Of course I won't forget about it, but I'm not going to let her have the satisfaction of thinking she can ruin our plans to be together for the evening. So you can stop looking so worried,

David," Sarona continued, smiling and taking a sip from the glass of wine she'd been toying with idly.

"Shelia didn't reveal anything about you I didn't already know. I think she was betting she could shock me with her petty revelations of your less than stellar reputation. What she doesn't know is that I've discovered more about you in a few short days than she could ever know. Sure, there's no doubt you're a walking definition of the word 'playboy.' It's an image you've perfected and personified. But in your defense I have to admit I've learned there's more to you than just another pretty face," she teased. "In light of our stimulating conversations and your creative use of those moments when there was *nothing* to say, I've decided that you may have some redeeming qualities after all." Sarona chuckled. "In spite of your scandalous reputation."

He was relieved to hear her joke about his questionable character. It meant she hadn't let Shelia get to her and give her reasons for second thoughts about where they were headed. He relaxed and breathed easier, and settled into the meal and the remainder of the evening, enjoying the night as it was intended, talking, laughing and getting to know each other.

Chapter 7

They stood in front of Sarona's suite. He leaned around her to open the door and lightly brushed her arm as he reached for the handle. Then he stopped and reached for her instead, pulling her to him, hard and insistent.

Sarona silently watched as his face and lips slowly descended toward her. Time stood still as her lungs refused to breath and her mind went totally blank. The feel of his full, soft lips on hers was heart-stopping. His tongue teased and swept across her lips. His mouth, soft and firm, covered her mouth with a persistent and demanding need for entry, and she opened to receive him. His tongue delved, stroked, and cajoled to elicit a moan of pleasure from deep within, and her ears scarcely recognized the sound as her own pent up passion.

Her arms automatically reached to draw him closer, hold him tighter. Her body, held tightly against his, came into direct contact with the long, hard length of him, pressed firmly in the cradle between her legs. He pressed her body back against the door as he took the kiss deeper. One hand reached to cup her rounded bottom and pull her tighter against his hard arousal while the other hand held her head still for the invasion of his tongue.

The kiss seemed to go on forever until the need to breathe forced them reluctantly apart. David pressed little butterfly kisses along her lips, her throat and jaw. His tongue gently laved and caressed her ear lobe as his warm breath teased the lose tendrils of her hair. His voice, husky with lust and need, whispered suggestively in her ear, "Why don't we move this inside where we can be more comfortable?"

"Umm?" was her barely audible response.

"I said, why don't we move this inside where we can be more comfortable?" he repeated.

Sarona pulled back. Looking up, she immediately felt the sensation of being pulled, falling and drowning, into those irresistible brown eyes.

Gently stroking both cheeks with his thumbs, he asked, "What do you think, Sarona?" His eyes were searching, wary with concern, awaiting her reply.

Here it is, she thought, *the moment I've both dreaded and longed for. There's no more time to waste with uncertainty or self-denial. It's time to decide. It doesn't matter if it's just for tonight. Just for tonight will be enough. Tomorrow can take care of itself.* Sarona reached up and stroked his face, letting her fingers trail his jaw line to his mouth, then slide lingering caresses along his lips.

"What do I think?" she softly whispered, still entranced from his touch, intoxicated by his scent, and spellbound by the perfection of his full, soft lips. "I think you're a fantasy. A figment of my imagination contrived to haunt me, to make me long for impossible possibilities. It was a lie, you know? I pretended not to see you, and to seem uninterested. It was a precaution, my poor attempt at self-preservation, because I knew then what I know now; you would flood me with terrifying desire and passion, and I would drown in the deluge."

With her eyes fixed upon his lips and her mind finally made up, she smiled her decision. "Yes, David." Her eyes sparkled with anticipation. "Why *don't* we take this inside?"

He didn't hesitate. He reached for her key card and quickly unlocked the door, pressing her body backward into the room. His arms entangled with hers, he pulled her against him and held her close, pushing his face against her neck and inhaling deeply to breathe her in.

"I want you, Sarona," he said with his face still buried in the crook of her neck, his lips skimming the skin just below her ear. "I've wanted you for a very long time; maybe not since day one, but pretty damn close. You've always represented a challenge to me. I freely admit that in the beginning it was purely sexual, because let's face it, you are one hot, attractive, sexy lady. You turn heads, fire a man's imagination, and feed fantasies you don't even know about."

Sarona practically choked on her laughter as she blurted out, "You've got to be kidding! Where would you get an idea like that? No one sees me that way!"

He touched her cheek, gently letting his fingers slide across her soft, full, protruding lower lip. He sighed and gave her a look that stirred her soul. "Sarona, everyone sees you that way, trust me, I know, I'm a man. Just because *you* don't see it doesn't mean it isn't so."

She allowed him to draw her near, press the entire length of his body against her own, and cradle her in his arms. His arousal was apparent, his touch was gentle, and his caress so tender that she was once again sinking into sensation, drowning in desire, falling into fantasy, and positively purring with expectation.

"So, this is what it's like," she mused aloud, leaning back to give an intense and inquiring look into those oh-so-expressive-and-captivating eyes.

"What?" he asked, his responding stare just as intense, just as inquiring.

"Riding a roller coaster and losing yourself in the thrill of the ride…trying to catch your breath only to find there's no air way up there."

He smiled, a genuine smile tinged with a hint of laughter that slowly turned serious. "You take my breath away every time I look at you. You make me ache."

She smiled at his admission and took his hand and laid it upon her breast, and softly said, "Please, David, don't let tonight be part of some game. Play your game another time, but tonight...let tonight be something special. Let tonight be just for me."

"It's not a game, Sarona," he whispered back, "and if it were, this time I'm not playing it simply to win. This time I'm playing for keeps. I don't want it to end. You're my obsession. I can't think straight anymore because of you. There's hardly a minute in the day that I don't think about you. I can't get you out of my mind. Believe me, I've tried."

Capturing her face in both his hands, allowing her to see deep inside his soul, he continued to pour his heart into his words. "I won't lie and say this has nothing to do with sex because yes, sex is very much a part of what I think of, but there are so many things about you that excite me. You're smart, beautiful, witty, and a hell of a conversationalist. You're honest, you have a wicked sense of humor, and you don't take crap from anyone. You make the whole getting-to-know-someone process fun. Believe it or not, I haven't been with a woman since I started pursuing you."

She reached up to capture his hands beneath her own. "David, you started this almost a year ago! Are you saying you haven't had sex in all that time?"

"That's exactly what I'm saying."

"But...why?" she asked, completely shocked.

"Why? Because I was tired of being the player and tired of sex without substance, but I didn't know it until I started having those all too brief but wonderful encounters with you. You whetted my appetite for more and made me hungry to explore beyond the physical."

"Wow," she whispered, awed by his revelation. "I had no idea."

"I know, and look how long it's taken me to get you to listen," he said with a wry grin.

Sarona smiled and took his hand and led the way to the bedroom, openly anxious and excited to take him into her bed, into her arms, and into her body. This was it, she thought triumphantly; it was time to see this man in all his naked glory and discover if reality could in any way live up to her imagination.

Standing next to the bed, he placed both hands upon her shoulders and, taking a deep breath, he slid his fingers beneath the thin spaghetti straps that held her dress in place, bending to caress, kiss, and gently tease the silky soft, brown skin he found there. His hands slid down her back and explored each toned muscle and lush curve.

"Did I tell you how beautiful you look tonight?" he whispered as his fingers found the zipper, skillfully unzipped her dress, and then eased the straps from her shoulders. He buried his nose in the hollow of her neck and breathed her in.

"Yes, you did," she responded with a soft, intimate chuckle, "several times over."

*

As the material slipped from his fingers, his eyes were treated to a vision of perfection, wrapped like his very own present in black silk and lace underwear. Her figure was unmistakably that of a woman, her proportions generous, and her limbs toned, firm, and supple— a pure manifestation of feminine power and strength. He took great care and pleasure in unwrapping his present and gazing upon her flawless beauty. She looked like a goddess, an African or Egyptian Queen. Tall, majestic, and magnificent in her naked beauty, made for worship, made for loving. She wore her nakedness proudly and stood before him confident, certain, and unashamed. Looking at her brought an unfamiliar emotion to his heart, a choking sensation to his throat, and an incredible ache in his soul that demanded he touch her, take her, and claim her for his own.

He sat on the edge of the bed still fully clothed. There was something unbelievably bold, erotic, and sensual about her nakedness while he remained dressed. He wrapped his arms around her waist and pulled her forward to stand between his legs as he laid his face between her full, soft mounds. His hands cupped her breasts, thumbs stroking back and forth over her rigid and protruding nipples. His tongue toyed and suckled first one, then the other, licking and teasing her and pushing her toward rapture and beyond. His hands and mouth worked in harmony to elicit the moans he wanted to hear.

Sarona threw her head back, exposing her throat in blatant invitation; an age-old call recognized in every species from mate to mate. She reached to explore, to take away and remove the offending clothing he still wore, bit by bit, layer by layer until he, too, was as naked as she. She took her time to taste him, using her tongue to lick and tease his lips, his ear, and his throat and seek out his sensitive zones of pleasure. Slipping her arms around his neck, she brought his face, his lips, and his body closer. Finally she kissed him, long and hard, and rubbed herself against him like a cat, purring her contentment, marking her territory.

In one swift movement David stood, and they were face to face and skin to skin, the hammering of their hearts beating as one. He pulled her upturned face to his and delivered a kiss that left Sarona trembling in his arms. Reluctantly releasing her lips, he gently turned her body, wrapping himself around her like a blanket, fitting her back to his chest and pulling her bottom snugly against his groin. His cock, hard and solid, pressed tight against the cleft of her buttocks, and his arms embraced her and anchored her there as though he'd never let her go.

His hands and fingers began a slow, sensuous dance as they traveled and skipped lightly up and down her arms, traversing her body and skimming along the long, delectable length of her. He pushed his face close to inhale her unique and erotic scent and delivered kisses and licks to her neck, seeking out the hollow where it met her shoulder.

One arm draped across her breasts and shoulder and locked her in place while the other hand reached down to cup her mound. Fingers slid across her throbbing nub and dipped deep inside her wet and weeping sheath. Her body shuddered, and he reveled in her response. He pulled her tighter against his fully engorged arousal as it jumped and pulsed with instant recognition and need.

He saw their reflection in one of the many mirrors placed around the bedroom, and his breath hitched at the sight. He was struck by the contrast of golden bronze and natural caramel brown, and the beauty in the colors of their skin as they intermingled.

He lifted her chin and prodded her to gaze at their reflected image, to stare into his eyes that burned with the fire of a desire as heated as her own. His hand fondled her breasts, feathered over her nipples, and flowed across her body like liquid magic, leaving a raging inferno in their wake.

"You look so beautiful." He marveled at how perfectly she fit into the curve of his body, as though she had been fashioned just for him. "We fit, Sarona."

She smiled seductively at their reflection in the mirror and stretched both arms above her head to encircle his neck and pull his face closer to hers. The movement caused her breasts to rise and extend outward. She pushed her bottom back against his arousal and rubbed against him in small, sensual circles. Staring back into the depths of his eyes, a reflecting pool of brown honey, she softly replied, "Yes, David…we fit perfectly."

Rubbing and stroking her bare bottom from behind, he whispered in her ear; the sound of his voice seduced her as it thrummed and vibrated in harmony with the stroke of his hand.

"I know how to make love to the woman in you, Sarona. I know how to pleasure and please her...if she'll let me." Finally reaching a point where he was unable to stand the buildup of passion a moment longer, he expertly maneuvered them both onto the bed, where they landed entangled in each other's arms. He rained soft, tender kisses upon her face and down her throat and took his time licking and swirling his tongue on a downward path to her luscious breasts. He cupped both delicious mounds in his hands, teasing one dark nipple with his thumb and the other with his mouth.

She gasped and trembled. She excited him, stirred his passion, and fired his desire, elevated his need and his craving. She moaned with each swipe of his tongue and the tender brush of his hand, rising and pressing to bring her body closer and tighter against him. His hand slid lower, his fingers glided and probed and delved into her soft, velvet folds, then danced and teased across her sensitive clit, eliciting mewling cries of need and pleasure.

"Hurry, David," she pleaded, her feminine channel slick, wet, and whimpering with need, begging that he take her.

"I can't, Sarona," he murmured, his voice harsh from wanting. "I've dreamed of this, ached for this, and waited too long for this moment to rush. I'm going to take my time to find what gives you pleasure, what makes you moan. I'm going to taste you, savor you, and lick you up like melting ice cream on a hot summer's day. I want you to want me as much and as badly as I want you, and I won't be satisfied until I hear you scream my name."

He dipped his head lower and rubbed his face along her body, marking her with his scent and breathing her in. His mouth traveled the path of his hands until he reached his destination—the delicate fragrance of her sex and the doorway to paradise. He resisted the over-powering urge to bury his face there between her legs. He needed to take his time, to discover and uncover the key to her pleasure. His tongue glided, sought, and connected with satin smooth folds of flesh. He lapped, licked, and delved to taste the creamy flow of liquid nectar, oozing forth, generated by his touch.

"Ah, I knew it," he groaned.

"Knew what?" she asked in breathless wonder.

"I knew you tasted like caramel. Sweet, creamy caramel," he said, as he continued to lap and lick from her fountain of delight. "I've dreamed of your taste, your silky softness, and your smell," he said. "All are imprinted and imbedded like a memory I can't erase."

He continued his exploration, his mouth alternately gentle and demanding, seeking her sweetest spot. His tongue and fingers worked in unison, delving within her depths, probing and strok-ing, magically stirring, coaxing, and delivering exquisitely painful pleasure.

Her body writhed and rippled from the onslaught of his heat, and his scorching hot mouth and tongue pressed firm against her clit. It spiraled, licked, and speared her, skillfully and deliciously torturing her hot divide.

She was in mindless ecstasy. Her nipples taut, her body stiff-ened, tightened. Her hands reached to hold his head, grasping at his curls as she loudly whimpered and moaned the unmistakable signal of her approaching release, holding on to ride the tide.

He listened for and relished in the telltale sounds of her delight, her moans. He was pushed toward the edge with his desire to feel and experience her ultimate pleasure engulfing him. He grasped her hands and held them down to her side as he relentlessly, voraciously devoured her. His want heightened and intensified from her sounds of pleasure, and his cock throbbed and pulsed with excitement and anticipation. He was rewarded when he heard her keening wail and felt her shudder, tremble, and shake, and his name screamed from her lips as her orgasm overtook her...and him.

"David," she breathed in a voice weakened by her powerful orgasm, "I want you, I need to feel you, above me...inside me."

"And that's where I want to be," he murmured as he spread his body over her and moved into position to sink himself between the softness of her silky thighs, to take her and lay ultimate claim to her. Poised at the entrance to paradise, he paused to look into her eyes. He wanted to see and savor this moment, the moment of his possession, of his coming home to sanctuary. "Don't," he whispered, his voice filled with emotion. "Don't close your eyes. I want to see."

"See what?" she whimpered, barely able to comply, her eyes drifting shut as she rode a second wave of euphoria.

"I want to see the look in your eyes, the way they go dark and deepen with a secret mystery all your own. I want to be immersed and totally lost in that mystery, your eyes, and your body."

He pushed forward, and the tip of his shaft was instantly encased in velvet and bathed in liquid heat—soft, moist heat, intense heat that made him shudder and inhale sharply, the sound echoed by her equally breathy intake. He exhaled and pushed deep, stopped and enjoyed and reveled in the sensation, the exploration of the unknown. He withdrew and pushed deeper, and was engulfed in silk, tight, pulsating and scorching hot.

His body shivered as he plunged and sank deeper, pulled and gripped by her silken softness. Pumping his hips, sliding smoothly back and forth, in and out, he was instantly wrapped in mounting ecstasy with each slow, measured stroke. Engulfed in fire, he burned and ached with the joy and pain of such bliss, such delight.

She shook and trembled against him. She wrapped her arms and legs around him tighter, gripped and held him closer and moved and rose to meet his every plunge, to match each deepening stroke.

His mind and body basked in her beauty, her body, and the splendor of the moment. He was set upon his intent to give her pleasure and seal a place for himself in her mind and soul. He plunged hard, fast, and deep, over and over…reaching, pushing, and trying to get so far into her that she would never be able to get him out. He wanted more than her body. God help him, he wanted it all…her mind, her body, and her soul.

His pace quickened, his strokes became shorter as the rhythm of his motion adjusted to match her answering thrusts. Her silken walls gripped and squeezed him and pulled him deeper, toward that point of no return, and he went willingly, holding nothing back. He desperately wanted to hold on to the feeling, to hold back the tide, but she refused to let him.

He felt intense heat and the fire of his gut-wrenching orgasm blossomed and burned as it exploded and burst from his groin, traveling up to his head and down to his toes, stealing the very air he breathed. And she was with him, bursting and burning in her own volcanic heat and flame. Both were ensnared in a breathless world of heat and passion. His arms tightened as his body jerked and convulsed with shockwaves of indescribable pleasure.

They shuddered together in climactic aftershock, taking in great gulps of air to replenish oxygen-depleted lungs, each bathing and soaking in the afterglow and waiting for the sensation to subside. David turned and positioned them both on their sides as his now deflated shaft slipped from its haven between her legs.

He continued to hold her close, gently stroking her backside and breathing in their combined scent of sex, sweat, and surrender. Sarona snuggled close under his chin and gave a contented sigh.

"That was un-fucking believable," he croaked, his heart still rapidly beating and his voice strained from the force of his climax. "I don't think I've ever had an orgasm that powerful before," he stated, filled with awe.

"Ditto to that," Sarona responded, her voice no less strained and barely above a whisper. "My feet are tingling! That's never happened before!"

David chuckled at her response, "I hope that's not the only thing tingling." She grinned back and thumped him in the chest.

"Don't go getting a swelled head, Mr. Broussard. I'm sure it's just a problem with circulation. My doctor warned me that keeping my legs elevated too long could cause a temporary loss of feeling in the lower extremities," she quipped impishly.

"Oh he did, did he?" His voice filled with laughter. "Did he happen to mention what the solution to this problem would be?"

"Yes," Sarona said as she pushed and flipped him over on his back and straddled his body. "He said I should spend more time on my knees."

Chapter 8

BEEP! BEEP! BEEP!

His eyes flew open, the sound of the alarm still ringing in his ears. He groaned inwardly while making a silent plea. *Please tell me this wasn't another damn dream.* His mind reeled with denial as his heart pounded with the feeling of utter betrayal.

He looked up at the ceiling, blinking at the unfamiliar colors and patterns. Movement to his left accompanied by a slender brown arm reaching across his chest made his heart stop, then start beating again. The hand at the end of the arm fumbled for the button on the alarm clock to put an end to the incessant beeping.

"Ahh." The muffled groan came from the warm, silky body of the woman lying cuddled next to him. "I can't move." Sarona groaned again. "I am completely and totally exhausted. I'm worn out. I don't want to get up."

David was ecstatic. *This was no dream!* Memories of the night before flooded him with immediate heat and desire. He was thrilled beyond words. It was true. At long last, his dream had come true. A grin spread across this face as he pulled her into his arms and wrapped her up tight. He didn't want to let her go.

"Let's not go to classes today," he whispered seductively in her ear. "Let's play hooky. I want to spend the entire day making love to you."

"Umm. That sounds incredibly enticing, but you know we can't," Sarona laughed. "Today is the final day, and we have to get our diplomas to prove to our bosses that we actually went to those boring classes."

"I'm a software genius. I can fake a diploma blindfolded," David said, nuzzling and nipping at her neck, trying to convince her to see the beauty of his logic.

"You present a tempting offer, oh, brilliant one," was her breathless response, as she nearly succumbed to the magical sensations from his velvet tongue. "But need I remind you forgery is a federal offense, subject to time in prison?"

"Okay, I'll grudgingly admit, you make a valid point about the prospect of prison, but I still think we can come up with a convincing reason to miss classes for the final day. How about a note from a doctor saying we're suffering from sexual exhaustion?"

"You don't seem all that exhausted to me." Sarona chortled. "You're like the Energizer Bunny—you keep going and going and going, and…well, you get my drift. Furthermore, I believe I'm the only one of this duo who would be justified in making such a claim," she said, her weariness suddenly evident in her voice.

"Are you okay?" David asked, suddenly serious and concerned about how she might be feeling. She was right; he had been nearly insatiable last night. The memory of their lovemaking was still fresh in his mind. He hadn't been able to get enough of her luscious body wrapped around his, the feel of her soft silky skin beneath his fingers and his lips or how she'd willingly and without hesitation come into his arms each time he'd reached for her throughout the night. And he had reached for her often.

Despite his rumored and unwanted reputation about his many sexual encounters, he'd never experienced such passion and excitement before. Sex had always seemed a one-sided affair for him. There were plenty of women willing to take what he offered, but few had satisfied *his* needs. Few could quench the fire that burned him from within.

Sarona was different. She made love without reservations, without holding back—unselfishly. She'd met and matched his passionate aggression with an equally voracious appetite, kiss for kiss and stroke for stroke. She'd been open and receptive to him in every way. His body trembled, and his cock stiffened and pulsated with the memory. Her mouth and hands had played him like an instrument, expertly stroking and plucking his chords to elicit that elusive perfect pitch. Her mouth had been a cavern of heat, the silken stroke of her tongue on his cock sent wave after wave of sensation spiraling, cascading throughout his body. His hips had lifted in mindless obedience to meet every stroke of her hand, pull of her mouth, and rasp of her tongue as though he were a marionette moved at the will of the puppeteer. He was on fire, engulfed in flames; he burned with lust, desire and pain. She had been relentless in her pursuit of his surrender, and he had succumbed to her will, over and over again.

"I'm fine, David," he heard her say, her voice bringing him back to the present, "just a little tired. You have to admit, we had a long night."

"Are you sure? Maybe you really should consider not going to class. You could sleep in, rest for a while," he said, his voice anxious with concern.

"I'll be okay, David, trust me. Besides, today is only half a day—it'll be done and over before we know it. Afterward, I'm going to come back here and crash for the rest of the day. I'm going to need my rest," she said in a husky voice, "because I fully expect to have a late afternoon visit from my overnight guest."

*

Just as Sarona had predicted, the morning flew by. The conference ended with the same flourish as it began, and then it was over. She glimpsed David in a far off corner of the room. They exchanged a brief, secret smile and then immersed themselves in the attention of others, taking care of last-minute networking and saying good-bye to colleagues.

By twelve-thirty, Sarona was on her way to the elevators when she heard her name called from somewhere behind her. She turned to see a woman whose face seemed familiar, but whom she was sure she didn't know. The woman approached, held out her hand, and said, "Hi. You're Sarona Maxwell, right?"

"Yes?" Sarona answered, wary about who the unknown woman might be.

"My name is Ellen Matthews. I'm one of the bystanders who witnessed last night's unbelievable spectacle with Shelia Preston."

"I'm sorry to hear that," Sarona stated, shaking the woman's hand in greeting, leery of where the conversation might be headed.

"I just wanted to congratulate you on the way you handled Shelia. I've known her for years, and I know she's not an easy person to deal with under the best of circumstances. Last night was an exceptionally sensitive moment, and I believe you handled the incident extremely well."

"Well, I tried to do my best to defuse what could have been a volatile situation."

"You did an admirable job, especially considering her insults were used to obviously provoke a response to make you look bad. Those of us who have been privy to Shelia's tirades in the past were impressed by your ability to effectively shut her up." Ellen chuckled. "Afterward, we were all gathered in the bar, talking about the scene, and following a few too many drinks, some of us actually broke out in song, singing like the Munchkins from *The Wizard of Oz*...loudly proclaiming that the wicked witch was dead."

Sarona burst out laughing and shook her head at Ellen's outrageous analogy of what Shelia's friends actually thought of her. She chatted a few minutes longer, then said goodbye and continued on to her suite.

When Sarona opened the door, she was greeted by the sight and fragrance of a room filled to capacity with beautiful flowers. Nearly every surface held a vase filled with a variety of blossoms. There were roses in every color, orchids, daisies, and chrysanthemums... a virtual explosion of blooms. Her eyes were transformed into wide, round saucers, and her mouth dropped open in surprise. She was shocked and delighted beyond words.

"David." She laughed out loud. "No wonder you're such a ladies' man. You certainly know how to say thank you!" She pulled a card from the nearest bunch and read: *I will think of you long and often, throughout this day...and I will long for you often, throughout this day, David.*

Still grinning from ear to ear, Sarona went into the bedroom. There, positioned on the bed, was a very large, white gift box, complete with an equally large red ribbon and bow. She excitedly opened the box and found what looked to be a beautiful, authentic Japanese kimono lying inside. It was black silk brocade with tiny white embroidered egrets in flight, scattered against a colorful but muted background of green and red. It looked like a painting in liquid silk.

She gingerly pulled it out of the box to hold it and let the material slip and slide through her hands. Her fingers glided over the silk, stroking the intricate swirls and loops of the exquisite needlework. It closely resembled a one-of-a-kind work of art. She smiled to herself, because somehow she knew David was a one-of-a-kind kind of guy.

With that thought still in her head, and wondering where he could have gotten such an expensive gift on such short notice, Sarona quickly undressed to try it on. It fit her as if made for her, and she looked absolutely gorgeous in it.

Admiring her reflection in the mirror from every possible angle, she paused when she heard a knock at the door. Thinking it must be David and still wrapped in her luxurious kimono, she practically ran to open the door with a big, welcoming grin, only to be surprised by the sight of a hotel service rep.

Standing in front of her was a cute, petite woman with short blonde hair, dressed in a white uniform and wearing a nametag that said *Hotel Masseur*. She was accompanied by a rolling cart, complete with table and an assortment of massage equipment and accessories.

"Good afternoon. My name is Maureen, and I'm here for your in-room massage appointment," the lady in front of her stated with a bright, cheery smile and a very British accent. Recovering from her surprise and disappointment, Sarona looked at the smiling woman in confusion.

"I'm sorry; there must be some mistake. I didn't order a masseuse."

"No, Ms. Maxwell, there's no mistake. An appointment was made this morning by Mr. Broussard, who stated I was to arrive here at precisely one o'clock," Maureen said as she pointedly looked at her wristwatch. "He left strict instructions that I was to bring the necessary equipment and an assortment of products to provide you with a wide variety of selection of oils, lotions, etc. for your massage. His exact words were. 'I want you to give the lady, whatever she wants.' I've brought a wide range of items offered here at the hotel, but if I don't have something you like with me, it will be no problem to have it delivered. He also left this note for you." Maureen reached in her pocket and handed Sarona a cream-colored, gilded envelope with her name written on the outside. "Now, may I come in and set up?"

In a state of shock, Sarona accepted the envelope and stood aside, opening the door wide to allow Maureen's entry. She watched as Maureen expertly maneuvered her cart and table into the bedroom where she could begin assembling her equipment. She then went straight into the bathroom and began running a warm bath, sprinkled bath salts into the tub, directly under the stream of water, and turned on the jets.

Sarona watched the practiced precision of her movements, still in a state of shock. Her mind was still assimilating the enormity of these several sudden and unexpected events. *God! The man is one surprise after another*, she thought as she followed the woman's every motion.

Suddenly remembering the envelope in her hand, Sarona anxiously tore it open and removed the hand-written note inside.

> *You looked so tired this morning, I was concerned and feeling a bit guilty…especially after such a wonderful and unforgettable night. So, to ease my conscience, I'm sending this gift of leisure and relaxation. Please enjoy, with the knowledge that you have my deepest respect and appreciation.*
>
> *P.S. I want you well rested for my return.*
>
> *David*

Sarona was once again grinning from ear to ear, lightheaded and positively giddy with joy. She'd never in her life felt so pampered! With this dawning realization, she reached her arms around herself and hugged herself as tight as she could, to keep from screaming at the top of her lungs. How was a woman supposed to take all this in without bursting at the seams?

Maureen handed Sarona a catalogue to browse, detailing the types of massages and their therapeutic value. While she continued to prepare the room and arrange her station, she briefly explained her qualifications. "I am trained in diverse styles of therapeutic massage: Shiatsu, Hawaiian Lomi-Lomi, California Deep Tissue massage and a variety of others. If you have a preference other than what is listed in our catalogue, I'm sure we can accommodate your wishes. If you like, we can also include a salt scrub to exfoliate your body, stimulate cell regeneration, and increase circulation to your skin.

"While I'm still setting up, I'd like you to get into the tub and soak there for about fifteen to twenty minutes. The salts and jets of warm water will relax your muscles and ease any residual tension you may have. You can browse the catalogue while you soak."

Sarona did as she was told and went into the bathroom and closed the door behind her. Maureen had dimmed the lights and turned on the in-wall stereo that piped in an odd but soothing combination of mellow jazz and the sounds of nature. She had placed a large, plush towel on the edge of the tub and an equally plush robe on the hook behind the door. There were velvet-like slippers on the floor in front of the tub. On top of the towel sat a white, velvet sleeping mask, and a bath headrest had been secured to the tub. Sarona slipped out of her kimono, pulled her hair up into a ponytail and pinned it to the top of her head, then eased her aching body into liquid bliss.

Twenty minutes later, there was a soft knock on the door, and Maureen peeked inside. The jets, the salts, and the warm water had done exactly what Maureen said they would. Sarona had drifted off to sleep. At the sound of the light tap on the door, Sarona opened her eyes. "I'm all set up and ready to begin. Can I help you out of the tub?"

"Thank you, but I'll be fine. I'll be there in a moment." Sarona sighed with obvious contentment.

"Have you decided what you'd like?" Maureen asked as she made Sarona comfortable on the table.

"There are too many choices." Sarona laughed. "They all sound so good; I'm not sure what I want. What do you recommend?"

"Well, ma'am, it would depend on what your body is telling you it needs. Are you tired? Do you have stress or tension? Are your muscles sore and achy?"

"Yes…no…and yes." Sarona answered her questions in order.

"Then I would recommend a deep tissue massage. It will be very relaxing and will rid your body of most of its aches and pains."

"Okay, then let's go with the California Deep Tissue massage. Does that come with the suggested salt scrub as well?"

"It can be included, if that's what you would like."

"I think I'll want that too."

"Do you have a preference of oils or lotions?"

"Oil, please. I like musk and exotic fragrances. Do you have something like that?"

"Yes, I believe I do have a selection of spicy musks from the Orient and Middle Eastern cultures. They can be vibrant and very uplifting."

"Vibrant and uplifting it is," Sarona said as she pushed her face into the opening of the table's head rest. If last night's exhausting trysts between the sheets were any indication of David's appetite for making love, she was going to need all the energy she could muster for the evening to come. That was the last thought in her head as the first sure strokes of Maureen's hands began to work their magic on her body.

*

"Hello. Dr. Jeffers' Office, how may I help you?"

"Hi Candy. It's Sarona. Is Joyce available?"

"Hello, Ms. Maxwell. No, I'm afraid she's with a client. Can I take a message?"

"Yes. I'll make it short and quick. Would you please tell her I'm happy to report that there have been shouts of hallelujah to the rafters. Full details to follow at a later date."

"Okay, Ms. Maxell, will do. It sounds like you're having a good time."

"Candy, girl, good does not come *close* to defining the time I'm having." Sarona chortled. "I'm living one of Joyce's famous episodes of 'life is an adventure!' I know I'm going to hate when it ends, but until then I'm 'Living La Vida Loca!'"

Candace laughed at Sarona's gaiety. "It sounds like you must have hooked up with Mr. Right!"

"Well, I wouldn't go that far, but I'll tell you what—he's the perfect candidate for Mr. 'Right Now!' Honey, I've got to run. I've got plans for the evening, and my time is running out. Just give Joyce my message and tell her I can't wait to see her when I get back. Oh, and tell her it's no wonder she makes the big bucks. Her advice is golden!"

Chapter 9

David stood at the door to Sarona's suite. He'd arrived accompanied by one of the hotel staff, who walked ahead of him pushing an elegant service cart covered with delicious delicacies. Having reached his destination, he tipped the waiter and sent him on his way, stating he'd take it from there. He had the silly hope Sarona would meet him at the door wearing nothing but the robe he'd had delivered, and he didn't want to share that vision of her with anyone else.

He'd spent the entire morning and most of the afternoon reliving every single moment that had led up to last night and today. He'd finally worn away her resistance—had torn down her wall and had beaten the challenge. He'd dreamed and fantasized for so long, had planned and waited for even longer, and now…and now here he was at her door, the only barrier left standing between them. He'd won, had achieved his goal, but during the process he'd reached a turning point so far beyond his expectations that there was no hope of going back to the way things once were. He couldn't even if he wanted to.

If he'd believed that, once he'd taken her body, the sensation of constant need and want would end or subside, he'd been dead wrong. He burned now more than before, and the feeling was brand new, as though his body had only just begun to come alive. He'd been in a state of continual arousal since early morning, as he'd watched her from across the room. Neither the time nor the distance had made a difference in how he felt; he still wanted her with the same heat and desire he'd experienced before he'd ever tasted her sweetness.

He'd wanted to give her more time to rest and relax and had waited as long as he could, until he couldn't hold out any longer.

He needed to be close; he craved her taste, her touch, and her wonderful mind. His light knock was answered almost immediately, as though she were waiting impatiently for his arrival. And she didn't disappoint him. There she stood, wrapped in black silk, more beautiful and magnificent than he had ever imagined. The sight of her made his blood rush and his heart pump with excitement. She took his breath away.

He pushed the cart straight ahead as he entered the room, and as the door closed he reached to pull her near. There were no words between them as he bent to take a kiss. She came willingly, without hesitation, pressing her body into his and leaning into his gentle embrace. The kiss was warm, tender, and filled with quiet desire. When it ended, Sarona snuggled close, resting her head on his chest, and he held her to him, thankful and content.

"I missed you," he whispered, nuzzling her bowed head.

"I missed you too," she said, burrowing closer and wrapping her arms around his waist.

"Um, I could get used to a welcome like this." David chuckled as he squeezed her tighter.

"Me too." She echoed his sentiments, the smile evident in the sound of her voice.

"In case you didn't notice, I've come bearing gifts."

"How could I not notice? The room is filled to overflowing. I'm basking in the glow of your gifts and wearing one of them as well. On second thought, make that two." She laughed softly. "One is the robe—the other is the new skin I'm in."

"You look stunning. I thought I could envision how beautiful you'd look wearing this, but my imagination didn't even come close." He touched her; he couldn't seem to help himself.

His fingers lightly brushed and followed the curve of her neck and drifted lower to stroke the inviting swell of her breast. He

sighed with pure delight, pleased to find her naked skin underneath. He lowered his head to nuzzle her neck; his tongue licked
her in the hollow he found there, and the moist warmth of his
mouth sent shivers cascading in waves down her spine. He became
more aggressive, more demanding, as his body melded and pressed
closer. She grasped his head between her hands, pulled his face to
her own, and kissed him hard, thrusting her tongue deep, swirling,
dueling, stirring his internal fire. Coming up for air, she put her
mouth to his ear and demanded in a husky, urgent voice, "Strip
for me. I want to see you take your clothes off. I want to see you
aroused, hard, and wanting me." His heart leaped and pounded
at her whispered command. He was instantly and unexpectedly
thrilled and excited at the thought of fulfilling her demand to
stand nude and compliant before her.

*

The moist warmth of his mouth sent shivers cascading in waves
down her spine and she basked in the feeling, letting it wash over
her. She allowed his exploration and permitted his roving hands
and mouth to devour her and pull her into a whirling vortex of
flaming heat and dark desire. Losing control and unable to take
the torture of his marauding mouth and teasing fingers any longer, she'd revealed her deepest yearning. She didn't know where it
came from, the unexpected and sudden need to say and want such
a decadent thing. She didn't know and she didn't care. This wasn't
the time to analyze. This was her time to explore, to feel and want,
to take and fulfill the overpowering need to indulge herself—in
whatever she wanted to do.

She was excited, wet with need and anticipation. He started to
undress for her. He took off his suit coat and tossed it aside, then

slowly and meticulously unbuttoned his shirt, letting it slide from his shoulders and drop to the floor. He wore nothing underneath, exposing a smooth, solid chest, arms, and shoulders displaying muscles that rippled with every movement. His hands glided down his torso, openly touching and exploring his body as they moved downward to the waist of his pants.

He unbuckled his belt and unzipped the pants, letting them drift low and hang at his hips. Sarona's eyes, eagerly watching and burning brightly, remained glued to the movement of his hands as they slowly unveiled and revealed his perfect masculine body. He was excited by her response and the look upon her face that transformed into obvious want and admiration.

She moved forward and rubbed her body against his, letting her hands rub and roam the length of him, his shoulders, arms, chest, abs…his crotch. She couldn't get enough of the combination of steel and strength that trembled from her touch. Her hand encountered the hard evidence of his desire and brushed his arousal through the fabric of his pants. She stroked and gripped his shaft and felt it pulse and jump in answer to her caress. She inhaled his scent. It intoxicated her, gave her a high as potent as any drug, and she took it in and let it take her over.

Reluctantly, she released her hold and stepped back to watch and wait. He resumed his striptease and continued to undress completely, stepping out of his shoes, pants, and silken boxers, dropping everything to the floor alongside his shirt. His hand encircled his shaft, his fingers stroking and rubbing it into hardened arousal. He watched her reaction as he played and pulled on his swollen manhood, and she stared at him without inhibition, open and shameless in her lustful gazing.

She reached out and touched his cock, to stroke and marvel at the feel of it—hard like steel yet smooth like silk and soft like velvet. Her fingers skimmed and stroked their way back and forth across the tip of his arousal and lightly brushed his erection and pulled gently upon his sac. She hefted the weight of him in the palm of her hand, reveling in the freedom to touch and travel up and down his length. Wrapping her hand around his cock, she gripped it, and giving him a wickedly enticing look, she pulled him forward and led him into the bedroom.

He dutifully followed. He was shocked to see the room's transformation. It was darkened and softly illuminated by candlelight and engulfed in a soothing, lavender aroma.

"You've been busy," he murmured as his eyes adjusted to the dimmed lighting and he inhaled the delicate aroma that wafted from the burning candles.

"Yes, I have."

"Where did all this come from?"

"Hotel gift shops come stocked with the most interesting things. You'd be surprised what one can find there," she responded absently, her eyes and hands obviously preoccupied by the sight and feel of him. "After receiving such wonderful flowers and gifts, you could say that I felt inspired. I wanted to show my appreciation, so I came up with a few ideas of my own."

She looked into his eyes and delighted in the glow she saw reflected there. It was his heat and his desire that spurred her determination to stir and rouse that glow into a raging, out of control inferno. Kneeling before him, she centered herself between his legs. She took his thickened shaft and rubbed it against her face, first one side then the other, and inhaled the pungent, sweet odor of his sex.

With glazed eyes he watched her stroke his tip and take the silky pearl drop of pre-cum she found there between her fingers to feel the texture of it, to taste and savor the tangy, semi-sweet flavor of him. She bent forward and took the tip of him into her mouth and lightly brushed it with her tongue. His head fell back and his eyes rolled up at the first, velvet-roughened rasp that glided across the head of his already painfully hard cock. She licked the tip and gently ran her tongue beneath the flared head, along the rim where head met shaft, then down the length of him, ending at those two glorious orbs.

Taking both into her hand, she massaged them softly while her tongue traveled back to the head. She took his engorged cock fully into her mouth to suckle and lick. One hand fondled his balls, and the other gripped his shaft and pulled him in and out of her mouth in long, slow, languid caresses.

"Sarona, babe, you're killing me," he groaned, "but I think I'll die a happy man."

"Mmm…you taste good." Her voice vibrated along the length of his cock. She continued her exploration, stroking, licking, touching, and marveling at the miracle of his still-growing member. She'd taken control and had become the aggressor, demanding and taking what she wanted, and he was willing to let her have her way.

She caressed and stroked his thickness and gently gripped and massaged his balls, enjoying immensely the feeling of total control and power and knowing she held the key to his pleasure in the palms of her hands. She slid her way up his body, and walking him backward, pushed him down upon the bed. Removing and dropping her robe to the floor, she stood before him once again in naked majesty, and once again the sight of her stole his breath from him. Joining him upon the bed, she straddled him and stretched his arms wide, holding them shackled above his head.

"I spent the entire morning and afternoon thinking about this, thinking about you lying beneath me and me having my way with you," she whispered, then nipped and licked his ear. "Touching your body excites me," she continued. "I'm going to seek out and find the most sensitive parts of your body and turn it into…one…big…erogenous…zone."

She punctuated each word with a long, lapping stroke from her tongue. "I want to feel it shiver and tremble beneath my hands and then shatter into a million pieces from your release when you come." She smiled with secret satisfaction as she felt his body's answering shudder of pleasure and anticipation. "Then I'm going to pick up those million pieces, put them back together…and start…all over…again."

Her lips and tongue traveled down his torso, lingering and teasing first one nipple, then the other. His breathy intake told them both that he was roused by her promise, and the pebbling and tightening of his nipples gave further evidence to his state of excitement. She rubbed and teased him with her large, swaying breasts; her hardened nipples, pointed and protruding, intensified the sensations of his already heightened senses.

"Last night I was yours. I willingly surrendered to your desire and gladly gave you everything you asked of me and more," she murmured as she continued her sensual attack, her tongue delving, tasting, spearing. "Tonight I expect no less in return."

She released his hands and commanded him to stay still. He wasn't allowed to touch her as she continued her unhurried assault upon his body. She licked, touched, stroked, caressed, and whispered to him continuously, sharing her fantasy with soft words and soft, deliberate touches. He groaned when she took his swollen cock into her hands and massaged it, stroked and suckled it.

She relished the feel of him, the smell of him…the taste of him. She breathed him in, held him close, and rejoiced in the beauty of his manhood—how it stood hard, high, and proud, anxious to be touched and taken. She teased him with her tongue, kissed him with her lips, and encircled him with her mouth, all the while listening to the sounds of his pleasure, the hoarse, guttural moans emanating from his throat.

She felt his body rigid, taut, and strained, writhing under the attentions of her experienced mouth and hands. She watched his fingers reach to hold onto the bed linens to anchor him through the onslaught of sensual overload, but she refused to give him relief, greedily seeking her own satisfaction, her own pleasure and fulfillment.

"Sarona," he croaked through clenched teeth. "I don't think I can take much more." His head was thrown back, his lungs taking in gulps of air as he fought to forestall imminent release.

She continued to bombard him with pain and pleasure, to stroke his body beyond endurance, until at last she could no longer delay her own need to feel him, hard and solid, gripped within her silken walls. Stroking and caressing him with one hand, she used the other to position his hardened cock as she moved over him. Taking her time, savoring the sensation, she slowly slid her wet, velvet sheath down his shaft and impaled herself with the length of him, the feeling so exhilarating, so electrifying, it took her breath away.

Sarona took control of the momentum and the movement. She set the rhythm and dictated the tempo. She rode him hard and fast, slow and easy, thrusting down and grinding her heated channel onto his hardened cock. She moved in a maddening up-down and circular motion, intended to drive him over the edge, beyond his control, and he willingly followed where she led. His compliance was total; he gave her his all and eagerly took and surrendered to the heat of her passion.

She met each thrust, every stroke, and rode each wave of pleasure as it rushed over her, through her, and she took him with her on that wild, raucous ride. His hands gripped her hips and held her tight as he rose to meet her downward, driving force. His heart pounded in time to the rhythm of her stroke, the sway of her breasts, and the grasp of her hands. They rode the tide together, took the plunge, and then crested the wave at the exact same moment.

His orgasm, her orgasm—their orgasm erupted and rippled through them, washed over them and carried them over the edge, and took them slipping and sliding blindly into blissful oblivion. It was an eruption of passion in its purest form.

Sarona collapsed and lay prone across David, weakened by her expended energy and that mind-blowing orgasm. David wrapped his arms around her and held her to him, his breathing coming in short, ragged gasps. Both were slick with sweat and speechless as they waited for their bodies to stop free falling and return safely to the haven of earth and reality.

"Oh, God." Sarona groaned, her head planted face down into the pillow beside his head. "I don't know about you, but I think if we keep this up, one of is going to keel over and die. We've got to stop this, or we won't survive. Have you ever heard of anyone actually dying from too much sex?" A hint of real concern colored the tone of her voice.

"No, I haven't, but God, what a way to go." David chuckled lightly.

"Thank you," Sarona whispered, her voice tired and drowsy from sexual exhaustion.

"For what?" David asked, his brow furrowed and his eyes staring blankly at the ceiling, clearly puzzled by her remark.

"For giving me my fantasy," she stated, as she slipped to his side and settled into what was fast becoming her favorite position, her head on his shoulder nestled beneath his chin, and slowly allowed fatigue and sleep to creep up and overtake her.

He rolled her over on her side and tucked her bottom into the cradle of his pelvis, spooning and cuddling her close. His nose was pressed against the nape of her neck, inhaling her scent once more. He wrapped his arm around her, and his hand cupped and stroked her breasts and nipples soothingly, lulling and beckoning them both into sated slumber. "Believe me, babe, the pleasure was all mine," he murmured in her ear as he too was claimed by exhaustion.

*

David pulled her to him, and nuzzling her neck, he circled her in his arms and began to gently kiss her awake. His lips were soft and teasing as he held her close. He breathed her in, profoundly aware of the significance of finding this remarkable woman lying next to him in bed. He closed his eyes and lightly stroked her soft skin, again marveling at its silk-like smoothness. Inhaling the heady aroma of their combined scents, he was instantly flooded with the memory of their night and afternoon together, making love.

He couldn't get enough of that scent, and he didn't think he ever would. He loved the feeling of waking up with her wrapped in his arms. His acknowledgement of the sentiment made him keenly aware of the subtle yet unmistakable change in him. A change that made him look more closely at the man he was becoming, evolving into in such a short period of time. A man who felt no shame in the fact that he craved the softness of a woman's touch, the strength of a woman's character, and the stimulation of her intellect, with the ability to let himself go to the possibility of being thoroughly loved and satisfied by one extraordinary woman.

*

Sarona awakened to soft warm kisses and the feeling of strong arms holding her tenderly. She felt the soothing, reassuring, and gentle stroking of nimble fingers and soft hands. She delighted in his touch, the memory of his sweetest surrender, and the thrill of finding him there, still in her bed. She was secretly captivated by his manner and the way he consistently treated her.

She smiled to herself, inwardly in awe at the contradiction of the perceived character and persona of the man—that a ladies' man actually knew how to treat a lady. That such a big, strong man could be so gentle. That such strength could conceal such tenderness. She loved that he was a sensual and sensitive man. A man who knew how to savor her body, touch her with fiery desire, and consume her with his lust. And look at her with eyes that left no doubt there was no other place in the world he'd rather be than in her arms.

His gentle touch, his warm eyes, and his demeanor conveyed admiration and respect. The hours she spent in his arms were the combination of when fantasy collided with reality and the end result was indefinable pleasure. She reached up to let her hand rest upon his chest, to feel the tempo, the rhythm of its rise and fall with each measured breath. She began her own unhurried exploration—her own quest to seek out, to uncover and connect to the man beneath that hard shell. Snuggling nearer and sighing contentedly, Sarona gave up all thought and burrowed closer, deeper into the safety of his hard, muscled strength and the sanctuary his arms willingly offered.

They both continued to lie quietly in each other's arms, each in their own world. No words were spoken. There was no need for words, for the silence between them spoke volumes.

Chapter 10

The bathroom was dimly lit by candlelight that spilled over from the bedroom, as well as a few candles placed sparingly throughout the room. Soft strains of romantic jazz wafted from the nearby stereo. The tub was filled to capacity with fragrantly scented water and bubbles.

"This was a wonderful idea, and I'm so glad I thought of it," Sarona cooed as she lifted one bubble-covered leg and rested a perfectly manicured foot upon David's chest. "I love bubble baths, and this tub is so huge, it's perfect for two!" She giggled with glee.

David laughed softly at her obvious happiness, deeply thrilled he was a part of it. Being together the last couple of days like this, sharing intimate moment after intimate moment, went far beyond his greatest expectations. He couldn't believe how incredible the time had been, bonded together, embraced in breathtaking passion for the past twenty-four short hours. Every minute with Sarona was a whole new experience for him, and he loved every minute. He didn't think he'd ever recover. He grinned broadly as he took the foot that rested upon his chest and began a slow, sensuous massage.

"Did I tell you how wonderful my massage was today?" she inquired with brightly sparkling eyes and a wide, playful smile.

"Yes, you did," he responded, looking intently at her foot, pretending to be particularly interested in her little toe.

"Did I tell you that I *loved* my massage today?" she asked in an overloud voice, trying to get his attention and have him look her in her eyes.

"Yes, you did," he replied again as he lifted her foot and kissed the arch, letting his tongue run up the ball of it and over her big toe before he took the end of it into his mouth and suckled it.

"Hmm." Sarona sighed with a little shiver. "Did I tell you I loved the flowers and the kimono?" she breathed.

"Yes, you did, and you did it in such an ingenious and original way." He chuckled at her response to his sensual teasing as he continued to kiss and nibble at her foot and toes.

"Did I tell you I've loved every minute we've spent together since last night?" she asked in a lowered voice.

"No," he said in an equally low voice. "That's one admission you've managed to keep to yourself."

"I have, you know. Loved every minute we've spent together since last night," she repeated, her playfulness suddenly and quietly giving way to the somber revelation.

He registered the change in her voice and raised his head to catch the look in her eyes. Sarona gently tugged at her foot and slowly withdrew it from his grasp, letting it glide a path down his chest and stomach before she slipped it back into the water by his side. Her eyes retraced the movement of her foot and came to rest on a spot in the middle of his chest. She raised her gaze, looking him solemnly in his eyes, and asked, "Do you wonder how we got here, David?"

David returned her unexpectedly melancholy stare, his heart suddenly in his throat because he didn't know where the question had come from and was immediately wary of where it might lead. He didn't like that all-too-thoughtful look on her face; he didn't want her to think too hard, to delve too deep, to go too far and break the magic spell that had been woven about them. "Here" was what he'd waited far too long for. "Here" was what he'd dreamed of and hoped for. He didn't want doubts or second thoughts to creep in and destroy the fragile foundation they were building.

"What do you mean?"

"You know what I mean. Look at us. It's been what, five days? How did we come so far, so fast? How did we go from casual conversation to intimate relations; how did we go from just for laughs to…bubble baths?"

He didn't know where she was going with this line of dialogue, and from the sound of it he didn't think he was going to like it. He leaned forward and took both her hands in his and held them to his lips, purposely kissing each finger.

With an intent look he said, "It shouldn't be that much of a mystery, Sarona. Sure, it's been five days, but we've known each other a lot longer. It's not like we're total strangers. This happened like these things typically do—boy meets girl, boy likes girl, boy chases girl until, in your case, she gets fed up and allows him to catch her. I know the line got crossed and things shifted from their expected path, but nothing in life stays the same. People and situations change. I can't tell you *how* we managed to get here, and frankly I don't care about the how of it. I'm just glad we did. Our being together is not totally by accident. Nor is it totally by design, but whether you call it fate or destiny I believe both had a hand in the orchestration of what I choose to think of as my good fortune. The last twenty-four hours have been the best-spent hours of my life. And, I know I'm not alone in this, Sarona. I know you've enjoyed it too, so don't you dare start tearing it apart by over examining and over analyzing and talking yourself into regretting this," he said with a hard, steely look in his eyes.

"That's not what I'm doing, David," she said with a small laugh. "I'm just curious as to how we came to be here, in this moment. This is totally out of character for me. And, if my past observations tell me anything, they tell me it's certainly out of character for you." She looked straight into his eyes, her eyebrows lifted expectantly.

She doesn't trust me, he thought, suddenly aware of the mixture of doubt and suspicion that rested upon her face, and that he heard echoed in her voice. *She doesn't trust this thing that's happening between us.* David reluctantly released her hands and slowly reclined back into the tub and crossed his arms over his chest. His eyes became hard and narrowed, and his jaw tightened as he pinned her with a penetrating stare.

"This isn't a question about how *we* got here, is it? You're wondering how *I* got here, and why. You're looking for the answer to the shift from my usual taste in women—to why I've pursued you, aren't you?"

To her credit, she wasn't intimidated by his stare, and she didn't wither or back down from the question. "Yes. That's exactly what I'm asking. What is the reason behind this change in preference? Why has your fondness for a certain type of woman taken such an extreme turn? Why are you suddenly interested in a voluptuous, full-figured black woman, instead of your usual skinny, white model type?"

"Like I said, people and situations change," he responded with a slight edge to his voice. "I told you, Sarona, I've done a lot of changing in the last year. It's something you wouldn't know, because you've never really *seen* me. I took a long, hard look at myself over the past year, and decided I didn't like what I saw or what I had become. I decided to make a change. Part of that change was to stop ignoring the fact that I am attracted to you."

David was slightly annoyed at her questions and the implication that she obviously believed his attraction might be based on her race. But he couldn't really blame her for her questions or her doubt; again, it was his track record with women that spoke louder than his words.

"You're right—I've always gravitated toward the thin, attractive blonde model type with more surface than substance. I suppose it was because I had no real desire to know what lay beneath that surface. Wanting to know what was on a woman's mind wasn't part of my agenda. I didn't date women for their minds; my interest was strictly physical. I lived a superficial life with superficial expectations. It was a choice."

Sarona said nothing and waited for him to continue.

"The women I've met in the past were as superficial and shallow as I was, and we were always a perfect match until I began to change; until I began to see the world around me and feel as though I was missing something. Maybe it's because I'm older now and a little more mature. Maybe it's because I grew tired of the superficial. Maybe it was a lot of things that I can't exactly put a label to, but at some point I realized the physical didn't matter as much…and it was no longer enough. You probably won't believe this, but you had a great deal to do with this change in me. There was always something about our periodic meetings and recurring tête-à-tête that intrigued and fascinated me. You're not an everyday, average kind of woman, Sarona. You're a challenge to a man's intellect and ego, and definitely not for the weak-minded or faint of heart. Whether you know it or not, there's something about you that demands notice and attention. And you got my attention. Your intellect and attitude separate you from the rest and serve notice to a potential suitor or lover that if he wants to be with you, he'd better bring his best and leave his ego behind."

He leaned forward slightly to look directly into her eyes and said, "The funny thing about change, Sarona, is that it's not conditional, nor is it limited in scope, so there's no telling what it will affect. It can occur in any shape and form—lighting fast or over a period of time—and it's obvious to me that your 'shape and form' falls within this unlimited scope. Perhaps this change has occurred too quickly, or too soon for you to be comfortable with...but for me it's taken a lifetime."

Still delivering an unyielding stare, David broached the subject he felt was at the heart of her questions and apprehension. "I'm not sure where these questions are coming from, but I think that on some level you believe Shelia's comment has merit. You think I'm here for curiosity's sake or to explore a myth. But you're wrong. This thing between us has nothing to do with your being black and me being white, but everything to do with a physical and mental attraction. Of course you're black, but first and foremost you're a woman; a woman I'm extremely attracted to, and who makes my blood boil at the sight, sound, and scent of her. I'm attracted to your beauty, your strength, and your no-nonsense attitude. And yes, I'm attracted to the color of your beautiful skin, but it's not for the sake of curiosity. My obsession isn't with the color of your skin, Sarona—it's with the woman, the total package. I won't even pretend that I know what the difference in our skin color can make in a relationship that could develop between us. But there's one thing I do know. I know there's nothing in life that I'm more willing to do than find out."

He reached out and took her hands and gently pulled her over to his side of the tub to cradle her in his arms. He brought his arms around her body and pulled her back against his chest. David pressed his face into her cheek and delivered several tiny kisses all along the side of her neck and face. Though he didn't know how, he was intent on convincing her that his reasons were motivated by nothing less than pure attraction and desire. He didn't want her probing the subject any further. He was afraid that if she looked hard enough, she would find a reason to end this budding relationship before it had a real chance to flower and bloom into something wonderful.

"I don't know how we got here, Sarona. I don't care how we got here. I'm simply grateful it was a short trip, and in spite of the bumps and pitfalls along the way, we finally arrived."

She settled into the circle of his arms and leaned her head back against the hardened muscle of his shoulder, releasing a soft, uncertain sigh. "I have enjoyed every moment with you, and I am grateful. Really, I am. What woman wouldn't be? You've been wonderful, attentive, sensitive, and sweet. I'm sorry if my questions suggest that I have doubts, David, but I'm afraid it's my nature to question things, and I can't help but question this. You have to understand that to me this is sudden and utterly unbelievable. To go from a state of barely knowing one another to…to flowers, massages, and exquisite gifts is absolutely unheard of. It's like a scene out of *Pretty Woman*. This is nothing short of pure fantasy."

Maybe he'd gone too far. Maybe his extravagant display had scared her. He'd only wanted to please and pamper her and make her feel special because she'd made him feel special. Considering her suddenly apparent suspicions and questioning of his motives, he probably should have stopped with the flowers.

With a small sigh, David rested his chin upon her head and wrapped her tighter in his embrace. He didn't want any more doubts. He didn't want any more questions, but he gave in to her concerns because he thought he understood her hesitation.

"Question all you want, Sarona, as long as you come up with the right answer." His voice was a hoarse whisper to her ears.

"Which is?"

"This is how it is, this is how it's supposed to be, and this is where you belong. Right here, right now, in this moment…with me."

They remained in the water for a short while longer, hugging, embracing, and drifting into conversation of a less serious nature, until they both agreed it was probably time to get out. David got out of the tub first and dried himself off with one of the plush towels, expertly folded and placed on the bathroom shelf, and wrapped it around his waist. Next, he reached to help her from the tub.

As she stood before him dripping wet, he took up the extra towel and proceeded to gently towel her body dry. He stood behind her, and beginning with her neck, shoulders, and arms, he gracefully brushed the towel back and forth in long, sensual strokes. He toweled her back and placed soft, lingering kisses upon her neck. His hands moved maddeningly slow in a concentrated motion as he began in earnest his self-appointed task to wipe her body dry from head to toe. Upon reaching the top of her full, round bottom, with a slow, measured, downward swipe he followed the shape of it with the towel, smoothing and cupping it intimately, possessively. He stroked her body at leisure as he meticulously worshipped her with the towel. He followed the curves of her body, down the length of her frame, intimately attending to every dip, crevice, and hollow. He was aroused by the look and feel of her skin beneath his hand and intoxicated with his desire for her.

Moving to position him in front of her, and with the same unhurried pace, he continued his task. He dried her breasts, softly brushing across her nipples and lifting each beautiful mound to wipe away the moisture underneath. He administered continual strokes across her stomach and down her arms with the same attentive care. He dropped to his knees and rubbed the towel up and down her legs, drying her hips and inner thighs and then moved to her mound, intimately stroking her there between her legs, lightly brushing across her sensitive nub with the back of his hand.

He leaned forward and delivered soft, intimate kisses along her inner thighs and licked her in the creases where leg and mound joined. He pressed his face forward, full into the divide between her legs, and inhaled deeply, taking in her scent to imprint upon himself her unique and tantalizing aroma. He craved the smell of that wonderful, spicy, warm, wet, turned-on scent.

His tongue darted out to sweep up and across her nether lips and suckle her button of pleasure. She groaned and placed her hands on his shoulders to steady herself.

David stood and draped the towel loosely around her hips. Standing between her legs, he gently but insistently pushed her back toward the marble counter, his arousal apparent as it lifted his towel and stood straight out in front of him. He nibbled at her neck and kissed and suckled her breasts as he continued to move forward, urging her back against the counter.

He loosed the towel at his waist and let it fall to the floor and without a single word made his intentions known. He wanted her on top of the counter, her legs spread and open to him. He wanted to taste and take her. He was seducing her all over again. He wanted to empty her mind of all doubts, questions, and concerns. For this moment, he wanted to fill her with his need, swamp her with his desire, and engulf her in his hunger for her.

He easily lifted her onto the counter, and the towel at her hips became a cushion. He stood there, comfortably nestled between her legs, legs that automatically rose to encircle him and hold him to her, firmly in the juncture between her thighs. She felt the tip of his engorged member as it bounced and rubbed teasingly against her sensitive folds, wet with the pearly slickness of his pre-release, undeniable proof of his want.

"You're like Ghirardelli chocolate to me. Do you know why?" he asked, his voice muted as his hands gradually slid up her thighs to explore those magnificent curves, swells, and dips. His eyes half closed and burning with desire, he watched his hands as they slowly crept up and around the contours of her hips and over her waist, seeking a path to her breasts. Her skin was like silk, soft and smooth to his touch.

Reaching his destination, he cupped both breasts, one in each hand. His thumbs made concentric circles around her nipples, soothing and stroking and causing delicious trembles and shivers throughout her body.

"Because," he continued in that same quiet voice, "like Ghirardelli chocolate you're indescribably delicious, smooth, decadent, and sweet—and completely irresistible. You have so many flavors you make my mouth water at the thought of tasting you," he whispered as he lowered his head, and his mouth took the place of one of his hands. His tongue laved and suckled one breast while he pinched and tweaked the nipple of the other, eliciting those soft moans of enjoyment he loved to hear.

He let the palm of his free hand slide lower to press, brush and rub over her clit as he slipped first one finger, then two, into the silken divide and encountered a hot pool of wetness there. David groaned and nearly went weak in the knees with his discovery. Her scent was erotic and overpowering and, the warm stream of moisture that coated his fingers made him virtually mad with need.

He withdrew his fingers and used his hand to guide and position his shaft at the entrance to her waiting, silky-smooth offering. He brushed the head of his cock against her, rubbed it over her sensitive bud and along the sides of her opening, teasing them both with the sensations of pleasure and pain—the pleasure of contact and the pain of denial. He held himself poised at the entry, with the knowledge that he was straining against wet, satin softness and reining in his need to mindlessly plunge deep into that velvet channel was pure torture.

His hot mouth reluctantly released her nipple and sought the fullness of her lips to explore the depth of her mouth and take pleasure in the taste of her tongue. When their lips touched and their mouths came together in a union of desperate passion, he could no longer deny his persistent and pressing need.

He buried his hands in her hair to pull her face to him. Simultaneously and in perfect sync, he thrust his tongue into her mouth and buried his cock balls-deep into her waiting offering of submission. The sensation was instant and explosive. She readily responded to his hunger and rocked into his intimate invasion, meeting the thrust of his tongue and arousal with a mindless fervor of her own.

She gripped him tighter between her legs, and the velvet-smooth walls of her inner muscles clamped around his erection and pulled him in deep, squeezed him tight. The feeling was so incredibly intense and so electrifying it felt like fire traveling from his scalp, down his back, and all the way to his toes. He craved the fire and welcomed the burn. He *wanted* to burn in the feeling of her inner depths wrapped around him, pulsating and twitching and driving him to the point of madness.

A rush of answering moisture flowed from her, engulfing him with her heat and drowning him in her liquid response. They held onto each other, tightly riding the shockwave of first contact, allowing their senses time to adjust to the exhilaration and the feeling of flight.

As he loosened his embrace, he withdrew his cock slowly and glided forward again slowly, creating a slow, deliberate, rhythmic pace. He eased her back gently against the wall and lifted her legs higher onto his arms, below his shoulders, allowing him to lean forward and push deeper. He nearly lost his control. He reached under her arms and gripped her by her shoulders as the motion of his body settled into the rhythm of rocking into her and out, slowly in and out, over and over, and again and again.

Impaled upon his impossibly hard arousal, she rocked forward to meet his driving force and danced with him to the sensuous dance of lovers, in time to the beat of the music his body made with hers. Together they dipped and thrust in perfect union, repeatedly driving forward and meeting in the middle.

Inevitably the constant friction of flesh meeting flesh and the ever-increasing hunger quickened the rhythm and accelerated the pace. Their bodies slammed together forcefully, loudly, the slapping sound of skin on skin the portent of mounting pleasure. Her channel tightened like a too-small glove and gripped him relentlessly, squeezing him beyond endurance and sanity.

"Oh, God," he stammered, as he ascended to the height of his passion and toward the peak of his control, his heart hammering against his ribs. She was with him in this ascension as they both struggled and strived to reach that point of no return; the point where control shatters like glass and glitters like diamonds, and emotions and senses clash and combine and become one unbelievable orgasm shared by both. They shuddered and crashed together as their passion melded into that one, magnificent moment of release.

"God, Sarona!" His breath came in ragged grasps as he tried to breathe through the rapid beating of his heart. He was weak from physical exertion and his orgasm, barely able to hold himself erect.

He released her legs and leaned into her, placing his hands at her sides to hold him steady. She leaned forward and wrapped her arms around his neck, her head resting on his shoulder, holding onto him for support. "I don't know if I can survive too many more moments like this," he tiredly rasped in her ear. "It just keeps getting better and better, every time we're together."

Chapter 11

"When did you have time to send flowers and pick out such an exquisite present?" Sarona asked, cuddled next to David, her body draped over his in contented repose. She'd spent the afternoon in deep, satisfied slumber; relaxed and rested, she had waited anxiously for David's return to her suite, to her bed, and to her arms.

His arrival had been accompanied by an elegant serving cart, laden with fruit and chocolate, more flowers, and an ice bucket chilling a large bottle of expensive champagne with two fluted glasses in fine crystal. They'd spent the late afternoon indulging in sweet, decadent delights, making love, by turns wild and wanton and slow and leisurely, uncovering, discovering, and reaching new heights, and christened every room in the suite from the bath to the balcony.

They triumphed in reaching the pleasurable heights of passion and exulted in each fantastic conclusion, yet nothing compared to the journey of getting there—the touching, talking and revealing of inner secrets. They had spent hours of mental, physical, and conversational lovemaking mixed with pure, fall-on-the-floor, unadulterated, wild sex.

"The flowers weren't hard to get, not when there's a concierge willing to do anything for a guest...and a generous tip." He held her close, her head resting in the crook of his neck, his hand traveling up and down her arm, fingers gently stroking in a soothing caress back and forth over her arm and shoulder.

She heard the pause in his voice and felt his fingers still in mid stroke.

"The kimono was something I saw months ago during one of my international trips," he said quietly. "It made me think of you—exotic, erotic, and mystical. I envisioned how I thought you would look wearing it. I couldn't help it. And before I knew it, I'd bought it. When I knew there was a chance I might see you here, I decided I'd bring it along and maybe have it delivered as an anonymous gift to your door. I never actually thought I'd have a chance to give it to you personally, but I dreamed of it. I told you, Sarona, you've been in my mind for months, and I haven't been able to let you go."

Sarona continued to lie at his side, digesting his confession. "I'll say one thing, David, being with you brings with it no shortage of surprises," she murmured, lifting her head to give him a long and thoughtful look.

"Stay with me, Sarona. Let's stay the weekend," David said, his voice deliberately magical, enticing, seductive; the heat of his breath teasing her ear and sending chills of anticipation down her spine. "Let's make love for hours," he coerced, "and immerse ourselves in raw, sexual fantasy and not come up for air until sunup Monday morning."

"It sounds wonderful," she breathed. "I've had the exact same fantasy running through my head since last night, but unfortunately I only have this suite through tonight. As it is, it's a good thing that the company's footing the bill; I can't afford a room like this for even one night. Well, maybe one night, but I'd have a hard time justifying the cost in my mind." Rising up on an elbow to look him in the eye, she impishly grinned and said, "You're good, babe, but not *that* good," then giggled in delight at the look that crossed his face.

David's eyes stretched wide as his eyebrows seemed to arch nearly to the top of his head. "Not *that* good?" he echoed in exaggerated disbelief. "Damn, I must be slipping." He again reached for her with sudden lust evident in his eyes. "I guess I'll have to work harder at improving my skills."

"Mmm," she moaned as his tongue glided across a particularly sensitive area behind her ear. "There's always room for improvement, I always say."

"Practice makes perfect," he murmured, as his lips and tongue traveled lower and laved each of her tightly budded nipples.

"There's no time like the present." She groaned, writhing under his wicked assault.

"Timing *is* everything," he mumbled as his tongue moved lower and his fingers glided across her throbbing clit.

"Less talk, more action," she gasped sharply at the first heated swipe of his tongue as he settled in to sip the sweet nectar gathering at the rim of her velvet cup.

"Your wish is my command," was his muffled response, and he had the last word as he dived in and proceeded to languidly lick and lap his way to heavenly bliss, pleasing them both.

*

"If you could, would you stay with me?" he asked.

"In a heartbeat," she replied without hesitation.

Looking at Sarona thoughtfully, David made up his mind and reached for the phone. He was taking a calculated risk, not knowing if his heart could take it if she misunderstood his motives for what he had done. "Front desk, please," he said in a calm voice, much calmer than he actually felt as he waited for the clerk to come on the line. "This is Mr. Broussard in Suite *La Amour*."

"Yes, Mr. Broussard, how may I help you?" the desk clerk responded.

"I'd like to extend my guest's stay for two days longer, please."

"Let's see, that would be Ms. Sarona Maxwell, correct?"

"Yes, that's correct."

"Will you be using the same method of payment?"

"Yes, please use the credit card you have on file."

"Will you need the other room extended for an additional period as well?" the clerk asked.

He knew the exact moment it hit Sarona. He saw realization dawn on her face, in her eyes. "I'm not sure yet," he said, eyeing Sarona warily, wondering what was going through her head. "I'll have to get back to you."

"All right, sir. I hope you enjoy the rest of your stay with us."

*

Sarona had watched and listened, curious at the exchange she'd heard over the phone. "Suite *La Amour*"…"Extend my guest's stay"…"Use the credit card on file"…

She stared at him, her eyes widening with sudden understanding. Her heart sank to the pit of her stomach and the breath caught in her throat, unable to escape past the lump suddenly lodged there. *Oh, my God! He set me up! The lying, low-life bastard son of a bitch set me up!* Her inner voice screamed the accusation in her head but she was too shocked to utter a sound.

Sarona stood and looked at him, her face and body flushed with anger and her eyes filled with fury. She was incensed and utterly speechless. Unable to articulate her anger in words, she snatched up her beautiful Japanese robe from the bed, twirled it into a ball, and threw it directly in David's face, then turned and stalked into the bathroom, slamming the door behind her.

*

David leaned back and slowly and repeatedly beat his head against the headboard, his eyes closed and his heart racing. He'd gone with his gut. Even though he'd known she wouldn't understand, she had to know. Things had gone too far. He could no longer allow lies and misunderstandings between them. Now that the lie was out, it was time to deal with the consequences. David got out of bed and crossed the room and stood in front of the bathroom door. Reaching out to turn the knob he found the door was locked.

"Sarona let me in."

"No!"

"We need to talk. Let me explain."

"You need to leave, right now!"

"No. I can't do that. Not until I tell you what this is about. Not until you listen to what I have to say."

"You know what, David? I think I'm done *listening* to you. You need to go now."

"Look, Sarona, I can be just as stubborn as you, and I'm not going anywhere until we talk, until you hear what I have to say."

"Fine, then don't leave," she yelled through the door. "After all, it is *your* suite, you paid for it. I'll go, and leave you to it!"

"All right, I'm leaving, but this isn't over, not by a long shot!" he yelled back through the door.

"Oh, it's over, all right, it's over and done!"

*

She listened to the sound of David getting dressed and gathering his things. A few minutes later, she heard the door to the suite open and slam shut.

"Good riddance," she yelled at the sound of the slamming door.

With her back against the door, her eyes closed, and her fists clenched, Sarona raged and vented in silence, so many thoughts and self-recriminations running through her head. How could she have let this happen? After everything she knew, everything she'd seen how *could* she have let herself fall for such a...*rogue?*

Fighting to get her anger under control, she reached within herself for an elusive, Zen-like calm, trying to find a center for her emotions and seek an escape from her feelings of humiliation and betrayal. Still fuming, she looked up to see her reflection in the mirror and was stunned by the image she saw there. It was clearly the perfect portrait of a woman who'd been made love to...thoroughly. She actually looked tousled, sexy and seductive.

She smiled unexpectedly, shocked at her own assessment, for she'd never thought of herself in quite that way before. She reached up to touch her still slightly swollen lips, tingling from the memory of his long, mind-drugging kisses. She stared at the undeniable glow of her complexion and the slight, telltale bruising here and there, evidence of their aggressive passion from two days of making love.

Her body shuddered involuntarily, her nipples pebbled, and her center became moist as she remembered in vivid detail his kiss, his touch, his penetration...his possession. The memory was so fresh, so powerful, she had to lean forward and place both hands on the bathroom counter to steady her swaying body.

Shaking her head to clear her mind, she grudgingly admitted to herself that David hadn't done anything that probably wasn't typical David. She'd known from the start he was a predator, constantly on the hunt for prey. He'd selected a target, set out with a plan, and executed it to perfection. He had wined and dined and romanced her out of her reservations...and her underwear.

That's what you get for not bothering to check out the rules before agreeing to play the game, Sarona laughingly thought to herself. *That's what happens when amateurs try to take on the pros...they get their ass spanked!*

"Bravo, Monsieur Broussard. Game, set, and match," she said out loud to her reflection in the mirror.

Opening the bathroom door, she was faced with the blatant reminder of those two days of mind-blowing sex. The rumpled sheets and linens of the unmade bed and the unmistakable fragrance of her perfume and his natural scent still lingered in the air. Wanting to avoid any further vivid imagery of the past twenty-four hours, she hurried into the living room to escape her memories, only to pull up short at the sight of David lying sprawled on the sofa. He was half dressed in slacks that hung loosely about his hips, and his shirt was unbuttoned and open, exposing his bare torso.

God! I was in bed with that? The man looked like a male super model, she thought, going weak at the knees at the sight of him.

"I thought you left," she said, her anger refueled by her body's response.

"I changed my mind. I told you, I'm not going anywhere until we talk."

"I have nothing to say to you," Sarona hissed, resentment still simmering just below the surface.

"It's okay, Sarona, the beauty of this is you don't have to *say* a thing. All you have to do is listen," David hissed back at her. Sarona, taken aback by his heated retort continued to stand where she was, her arms folded across her chest in obstinate defiance.

"Since it's late, I thought you might be hungry," David said as he sat up, his voice weary with despair, "so I took the liberty of ordering room service."

"Of course you did," she snapped sarcastically. "You're accustomed to taking liberties, aren't you?"

*

"As I said, I thought you might be hungry," David said evenly through clenched teeth. He'd waited for Sarona to emerge from the bathroom, hoping he could try and clear up the mess he'd made, that he could convince her to listen and allow him to explain. He knew she was upset—hell, upset was an understatement. If the look on her face and the sound of her voice were any indication, he'd say she was downright furious.

He didn't know what his chances were of getting her to hear him out but he was determined to try. He'd worked too hard, planned too long to get here, and though it was his methods that were in question, he'd do it all over again if it would guarantee the same outcome of holding Sarona in his arms.

Though it had been only five days, he'd experienced a lifetime in that short time. She'd made him come alive, opened up a world of emotion and feeling he'd had no idea existed. These few days together had given him a taste of what life could be beyond the self-absorbed selfishness of superficial sex, and he'd be damned if he'd go back to that one-dimensional existence, back to being in a world that didn't include her. He had to convince her this wasn't the work of a playboy trying to get another notch on his bedpost. He had to make her see there was something in him—in them—worth taking a chance on.

"Look Sarona, I know you're upset and hurt—"

"Hurt? Oh, please, don't flatter yourself. I'm not hurt, I'm pissed. I'm *angry* that I let myself be duped by the resident playboy!"

"Is that what you think this is about?" David bellowed. "Do you think this was some kind of trophy fuck? That all the time we've spent together was simply to add you to some nonexistent list of conquests for David the Conqueror?"

"Yes! That's exactly what I think this is about," Sarona heatedly replied. "If, as you said, I'm so damn hot, why else would you be here? I'm sure that laying claim to bagging such a hot babe has *nothing* to do with pumping up your already over inflated reputation. Aren't I the lucky one that you beat Bruce Carter to it? You may have more finesse, but at least he was honest and up front about *his* intentions. He made sure I knew from the start that it was straight up nothing but opportunity sex. I suppose I should have given Shelia more credit. It seems she knew what she was spouting after all about the Broussard Method. I guess I should be grateful you decided to end your charade; I could have left here with a false impression, thinking this really meant something," she said, flipping her hand out in a gesture to include the suite.

"I didn't do this for me," he said in frustration, spreading his arms wide to indicate the suite. "I did this for you. I wanted this for you. And yes, if I were lucky enough to convince you to be with me, I wanted it for us! I wanted to make our time together a fantasy, a dream come true...my dream come true. And if I never had more than this, I wanted to make this enough for the both of us. I know you feel used and lied to, and that's my fault, what my deception makes me guilty of, but it wasn't the intent. It was never the intent."

"I'm sorry, David, but I'm having a hard time grasping any other concept, so I'm afraid you're going to have to tell me. What was your intent?" Anger was still evident in her voice.

In a quiet and torn voice, David said, "Remember last night when you asked that I let our time together not be a game? That I let the moment be for you? It wasn't a game, Sarona. It was never a game. It was a mission! I've been on a mission for six months to make you mine, not for a game, not for a conquest, not for bragging rights—simply because I wanted you for me. This wasn't part of some method. I've never done anything like this before for anyone. I've never met anyone I *wanted* to do these things for. You made me want to pamper and spoil you, just so I could see the look in your eyes. If you like," he said tiredly. "I can give you the names of every woman I've been with, and you can conduct your own investigation.

"If I was able to pull it off, I wanted my time with you to be special, because you're special," he said, his voice now barely above a whisper. "If you never believe another thing I tell you, Sarona, please believe me when I say I have never been with a woman like you before. God, when I make love with you every time is like the first time all over again, and I can't get enough. You're like a damned drug, and I'm an addict begging for my next fix. I want to pull you around me and bury myself inside you every time I look at you, every time I'm near you, every chance I get. I've never experienced a connection like the one between you and me. I've never been with a woman who didn't have an ulterior motive, who wasn't using me like I've been accused of using them and am now being accused of using you."

*

Sarona grew quiet and calm. She listened to David's confession, but more importantly, she listened to how he put his heart into his words. She had set aside her feelings of indignation for the moment and slowly let go of her determination to hold on to her stubborn anger. She moved to sit beside him on the sofa, drawn by the pain and pleading evident in his eyes and voice. She sensed that he was desperate for her to believe him, and God help her, she wanted to.

"Why did you reveal this elaborate deception, David? Why didn't you just let me believe I had gotten this suite through a stroke of luck?"

"Because I wanted us to have more time together, and I didn't want that time to be spent under a shadow of lies and false pretenses."

"But it started that way—what difference would it make to end it that way?"

"The difference is, I had to do some deceitful and underhanded dealings to get you here, but I didn't want to resort to the same thing to keep you here. I want you to spend this time with me because you *want* to be here, and you needed the truth to make that decision for yourself."

Sarona looked into his eyes, searching for the truth, seeking the man beyond the reputation and the rumors. She'd seen him; she knew he was there because she'd touched his mind and brushed up against his soul, just as he'd touched her. She refused to believe he was anything less than what she believed. She wouldn't accept that she could be deceived and be so wrong about a man like David, the man he had allowed her to see, had stepped outside himself to share with her.

And just like that, she made her decision. Because she could no longer bear to witness his obvious suffering and uncertainty, she gave herself over to the feeling of forgiveness and handed him absolution. She reached up to brush an errant curl from his eyes, letting her hand slide down to cup his cheek. Bringing his face closer to her own, she stared deeply into his beautiful, whiskey-brown eyes and whispered with a sigh of resignation, "So, now what are we supposed to do? Kiss and make up?"

"It works for me," he said, his lips hovering close to hers. He closed the gap and kissed her lightly, hesitantly. She moved forward and deepened the kiss, and drawing him fully into her embrace, assuring him that he was forgiven.

David reluctantly ended the kiss, and holding her closely he buried his face in her hair. "I know I have a lot of strikes against me, and I've made a lot of mistakes. And, with my tarnished and imperfect reputation, it's going to take a lot to convince you I'm worth believing in, but I promise you this truth, Sarona, you're more woman than I've ever had," he whispered in her ear as he held her close and hugged her tightly, "and you're all the woman I'll ever need."

"Remember that the next time you piss me off," she whispered back, chuckling softly in his ear, with the tiniest hint of unshed tears in her voice. She wrapped her arms around him and snuggled in close and settled into what had now become her favorite position—her head tucked beneath his chin and her body locked within the warmth and strength of his embrace.

Sarona disengaged herself from David's arms and rose from the sofa. Taking his hand, she pulled him with her. "How much time do we have before room service arrives?" she asked with a naughty glint in her eyes.

"Since I didn't know how long it would take you to come out of the bathroom, I only put in an order from the menu. I told them to wait until I called back before delivering it. They're waiting for my call."

"Good," Sarona said. "That gives us plenty of time."

"Plenty of time for what?" David asked with a cautiously hopeful gleam in his eyes.

"Plenty of time to practice my waving," Sarona said with a decidedly devious laugh.

"Waving?" David said, his eyebrows knitted together, obviously not understanding her cryptic response and sudden impish behavior. She pulled him behind her as she led the way to the bedroom.

"Yes," Sarona said, momentarily distracted while picking through the fruit on the serving cart. She raised her hand in triumph as she picked up an apple and waved it under his nose. She then guided him to the bed and stripped him of his shirt and pants and removed her robe. Indicating he should lie down, Sarona straddled his naked body. Eyes sparkling with mischievous mirth, she said, "Now lie back and relax while I tell you a story about Adam and Eve...and an apple."

A Sneak Peek from Crimson Romance
From *Infamous* by Irene Preston

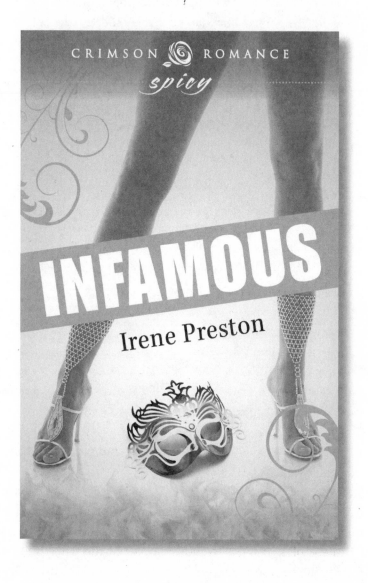

Chapter 1

It was Carnival in Venice.

Mardi Gras on the corner of Bourbon and Royal.

Tonight was pure Hollywood—and she was buying back in.

Jessica Sinclair stood in a scene straight out of one of her books—beautiful people, champagne, a posh ballroom in one of the city's most exclusive hotels. The entire room had been transformed for the night into a romantic Hollywood fantasy of Carnival, complete with backdrops of old-world streets and frescoed balconies. There was even the enigmatic hero—remote and aloof in black tie.

She spotted him the moment he entered the room. He paused in the doorway just as she looked up. For a second, all the sound in the crowded ballroom receded and it was just the two of them in a vast well of silence. Someone jostled her elbow, and all the noise and revelry crashed back in around her.

"Excuse me," she said to the man next to her. "I need to have a word with Kate while she's still coherent."

She spent the next hour circulating. Laughing. Chatting. Dancing. Through it all, her eyes found him in the crowd—as though he were the only solid thing in the room and everyone else merely butterflies flitting in and out of his orbit.

She grimaced at the fanciful thought. She was in an odd mood, but hadn't she come here to step, at least for the night, back into the fantasy? With her latest book off to the publisher, she was due an evening of indulgence. Only somehow, it was harder than she had expected to ignore the Styrofoam and spray paint and enjoy the pretty façade.

In the old days, she would have started the party well before she hit the ballroom and not counted it a success until every eye

, when she should be letting loose, she caught
y storing away information, impressions, and
ation. Half of Hollywood would give their eye-
arty, and she felt like the narrator in one of her
own books—an integral part of the story, but not an actual player.
She spotted a dark head in the crowd and felt a little frisson of
excitement.

It wasn't fair. In this crowd, he should blend right into the
woodwork. Was he even handsome? He didn't have the glossy
kind of image most of her male friends cultivated or even the
scruffy bad-boy look that was so sexy. His dark hair was cut in
a style that screamed boardroom rather than bedroom. Even the
Armani tux was the most conservative cut available. He should
have been completely unremarkable here amid the glittering
throng. Instead, he was the one who captured attention. Everyone
else seemed overdressed, overloud, and indistinguishable in their
glitz and glitter.

On one side of the room, her father, J.T. Sinclair, was holding
court. No champagne for him. He lifted his tumbler of scotch in
a salute as she joined him.

"So, Jessica, what do you think of my latest little project?"

"Little project?" She snorted. J.T. didn't have a modest bone
in his body, and he was fishing for a compliment. "You know
it's a huge success. The Carnival theme for the premiere and the
after-party was inspired. The reviews won't even matter once the
pictures hit the press—they'll be better than the trailers for public-
ity. Was it your idea?"

"Ah, well, if not, it was my genius to hire whoever *did* think
of it."

It took more than genius to pull off a success like this. It took
a good measure of power. In a town where you were only as good

as your last big hit, Daddy maintained a permanent rung at the top of the ladder.

If J.T. Sinclair had wanted the stars from his new movie, *Masque*, to show up at the premiere wearing sackcloth and ashes, every top designer in the city would have rushed to design sackcloth. Instead, the Carnival costumes were over-the-top glamorous. Jeweled masks and elaborate headpieces topped most of the outfits with gown designs ranging from opulent period knock-offs to risqué modern designs. Some of the men were a bit more restrained, but almost all sported at least a silk mask in deference to the theme.

She caught a flash of black and her smile faltered as she scanned the group of people a few feet away. J.T. was already turning to someone else in his knot of sycophants and she drifted away from him as she searched the crowd.

Close now. So close. Her heartbeat picked up just a little—an extra rat-a-tat-tat that she tried to ignore.

"Jess!"

An outrageously handsome face filled her vision. Blond hair and an impeccable tan blocked out any hint of sober black she might have seen across the room. She was swooped into a dramatic dip ending in an equally dramatic kiss full on the lips.

"Kiss, kiss, darling." Mason grinned wickedly as he set her back on her feet. Blue eyes glittered through his silk mask.

No boring black for Mason. The white mask with its gold trim matched the rest of his attire right down to the gold lace on his shirt. It should have looked ridiculous, but with his tousled hair and laughing eyes he somehow managed to look dashing instead. Utterly charming and photogenic—it was only part of what made Mason Knight one of the top male stars in Hollywood.

Mason snagged two glasses of champagne from a passing waiter. He drained his in a few gulps as she took a small sip of her own.

"Drink up, luv," he urged. "We are *celebrating*!" He waved the empty glass to encompass the room. "Another blockbuster hit for J.T., fame and glory for everyone. Why, I am practically guaranteed to double my not inconsiderable fan mail based on this one movie." He sighed theatrically and continued in a wide-eyed stage whisper. "They send *pictures*, you know. Thousands of pimple-faced teenage girls go to sleep every night dreaming of me—the only thing to give light to their lonely lives."

"Be nice, Mason. You know you live for the hero worship."

"Do I?" He swayed a little, as if considering the prospect. "Ah, Jess, you're right as always." He deposited his empty glass on a nearby table. Almost magically, another waiter appeared with more champagne. "Yes, indeed, what are a few white lies to gain the adoration of millions?"

She narrowed her eyes as he lifted the second glass and drained half of it in one gulp. Mason had the metabolism of a hummingbird. Despite his bad-boy reputation, she hadn't seen him really drunk in years. Tonight, his brilliant blue eyes were feverishly bright and his normally exuberant manner seemed too exaggerated.

Concerned, she wound her arm through his and tugged him toward the French doors at the end of the room.

"Come outside, we could both use some fresh air."

He leered down at her. "Trying to get me alone, darling? You only have to ask."

He followed her willingly enough, however. Another cause for concern. Mason generally had to be pried from the center of attention with a crowbar.

She managed to get him across the room and outside without interruption. As she pulled the door shut behind her, she felt the hairs on the back of her neck stand up. She glanced around to see if anyone had noticed them leaving, but J.T. was taking the stage for a speech and all eyes were on him. She tugged Mason away from the doorway and into the shadows at the edge of the balcony.

"Ready for a snuggle, snookums?"

She slapped his groping hand away and glared up at him.

"That's enough, Mason. What's wrong?"

He pouted at her over the rim of his champagne flute.

"You might as well spill it. You only flirt with me like this when you're upset." And never in private.

He sighed and the handsome rogue disappeared in the droop of his shoulders as he turned away from her. "They're all leaving me, Jess."

She was alarmed to hear his words slurring. "Don't be so cryptic; what do you mean?"

"Kit's going to New York. Broadway." He snorted. "Stupid, gay musical theatre, as if anyone wants to see *that*. Seven performances a week for God knows how long. And Susan, my sweet Susan has been making eyes at some pious frigging doctor she met at a charity event. He hasn't even got any money to speak of, just a lot of moral mumbo-jumbo about inner-city kids. She hasn't said anything to me yet, but it's only a matter time before she's reviewing the out-clause in the prenup." Mason paused for a little hiccup. "And here I'll be, alone with my adoring public. It's really too trite for words."

She slipped her arms around him, smiling into his back as she murmured, "Poor little rich boy, hmm?"

"Not funny," he muttered.

"No, I know. But Mace, if you think Susan has found someone else, have you considered…"

"No," he said vehemently.

"Well, you can't exactly expect Kit to stick around, then, can you?"

"Yes. No. Hell, I don't know." He twisted in her arms so he was facing her. "What am I going to do with myself, Jess?"

"Same as we've always done, live with our choices. If you don't like the ones you've made, make different ones."

He sighed and lowered his forehead to rest against hers.

"I've still got you."

She reached up to stroke his cheek, "Come on, Mr. Wonderful. Let's get you back to the party."

Just then the doors opened, their sheer curtains blowing out so light and noise from inside spilled onto the balcony. A tall figure stood backlit in the doorway, a featureless silhouette. She recognized him instantly. Her fantasy hero had finally caught up with her.

"Knight." His deep voice rolled out into the darkness. "I thought I saw you come out here. Your wife is looking for you."

From behind him, a slender figure pushed her way through the doorway.

"Oh, Jessica, thank goodness he's with you." Susan Knight wafted across the balcony to bestow a gentle kiss on Jessica's cheek. Her eyes sought Jessica's in the darkness.

Jessica patted her shoulder. "You know our boy, just a little post-wrap blues."

Susan smiled uncertainly at Mason. "Did you want to leave early?"

Instantly, the charming rogue was back.

"Jess is being a big mother hen. I have a case of Dom riding on what time Kate climbs on stage and wrestles the mic away from the band. Come along and let's see if we can give her a nudge in the right direction...."

Mason pulled Susan back into the ballroom. J.T. had finished his speech and the band was pounding out a fast-paced dance number.

Jessica turned away. Ignoring the other occupant of the balcony, she leaned against the balustrade and stared into the night. Spread out beneath her were the hotel's pool and gardens. During the day, a restaurant served breakfast and poolside lunch, but at this hour the tables were dark and only the gardens were lit. Tiny lights along the paths and through the trees gave the whole area a fairy-tale whimsy. A few couples strolled in the moonlight, but the summer heat kept most of the guests inside.

"Still quite the trio, aren't you?" Morgan's cool voice interrupted her thoughts. "Doesn't Susan ever get tired of finding you in Knight's arms?"

Jessica let the words drift past her on the warm air. Another time she knew they would hurt—sometime in the future when the odd magic of the night had worn off. For now, they simply floated past her, stray bits of sound, as she concentrated on the timbre of his voice whispering over her senses.

She lifted one shoulder in a negligent shrug, not bothering to answer.

*

Morgan sighed in frustration. Seeing her again was nothing like he had expected. It was worse and better in more ways than he could count. Tonight had started out as an impulse. Somehow he had never been dropped from J.T.'s guest list and he had been sure she would be here. But he had lied to himself about all his reasons for coming and now his penance was standing right here on the balcony with him, acting like she barely remembered his name.

He drank in her appearance in the moonlight. Long black hair cascaded dramatically down her back. Instead of plain elastic ties for her elaborate mask, strands of sparkling jewels glittered in the glossy tresses. Her blue and black gown dipped low in the back, exposing her pale skin almost to the cleft of her buttocks. She looked wild and untouchable—a fey princess dropped into the mortal plane. His fists clenched by his side as he remembered Knight's golden head bent close to hers. He had no use for fantasy, and he knew for a fact that Jessica was eminently touchable.

He moved closer, almost against his will, until he was just behind her—one hand on the balustrade, trapping her between his body and the wide stone rail. They were almost touching. Almost, but still a ghost of air whispered between them. Her perfume enveloped him, pulling him even closer. His head dipped to the hollow of her neck, and he allowed himself to inhale slowly.

It was a mistake. Her scent surrounded him like incense, dark and exotic. The balcony and the hotel disappeared, and a mélange of images assaulted him—his hands on her everywhere, silken skin sliding over his body, Jessica rising over him with the moonlight glowing on her pale skin as he plunged into the heat of her body.

Jessica turned, her breasts brushing his chest as she did. Her voice was low and husky.

"Come dance with me, Morgan."

She stepped past him and back toward the ballroom, not looking to see if he followed.

Like a fool, he did.

Inside, the party was in full swing. Lights flashed on the dance floor and the music throbbed. Around him, the cream of Hollywood swayed and gyrated—perfect bodies moving in perfect time with the pulse of the music. A blond starlet with an improbably round bosom clutched his arm. Luscious red lips pouted up at him and there was open invitation in the eyes behind the feathers and marabou as she bumped against him. He swept her hand aside as Jessica began to dance.

No one really looks like that when they dance—like the music was made for them, part of them. Sure, in the movies, but it's all editing and choreography. No one dances like that in real life.

But there was Jessica, right in front of him, yanking him into the fantasy. The other dancers, surreal in their masks and painted faces, melted into a kaleidoscope of color whirling around her.

He moved forward, irresistibly drawn to her. She circled, just out of reach. She moved with wanton abandon, brushing her body against his. He reached again, his fingertips just brushing the soft skin of her arm…And she was gone. She had to be doing it on purpose. Taunting him. Staying just out of reach. Just as he felt his control about to snap, the gods smiled on him and the song ended.

The lights dimmed even lower and the band segued into a slow instrumental.

He caught her slender wrist and yanked her against him. She gasped.

"Payback," he whispered. She shivered. He wondered if it was fear or anticipation.

She didn't resist, but closed her eyes as he pulled her into his arms. She twined her arms around his neck and allowed him to press the length of their bodies together. In her heels, her head fit perfectly on his shoulder. He could feel her warm breath against his neck. It was unbearably erotic.

His arms tightened involuntarily around her. He cursed, then surrendered to the inevitable. He shoved one thigh between her legs, cupped her bottom and pulled her against him. Instead of pushing him away, she ran her tongue along the pulse in his neck. Just a little flick, like she was tasting. He pulled her higher onto his thigh and she moaned and wriggled against his erection.

What was he supposed to be accomplishing? He couldn't remember any more and wasn't sure he cared.

He buried his face in her hair and breathed in the drugging scent as he held her hips against him. Then she was clenching frantically around him, her hands fisted in his hair. He was just about to go over with her when he realized what was happening and where they were.

He shoved her away.

"That's enough." He fought for control; fought to keep what he was feeling off his face. "I won't be part of one of your public scenes."

"In this crowd? We're hardly doing anything they haven't all seen before. It would barely cause a ripple if you stripped me naked on the hors d'oeuvres table."

Christ.

"Speak for yourself." He could barely manage to get the words out. "Exhibitionism isn't my style."

Jessica's gaze wandered down his body, lingered pointedly on his crotch. "Really? It seems to be doing it for you right now."

She stepped toward him, catching his lapels and pulling herself close to whisper in his ear. "You know you want me. Right now my panties are dripping…tonight, you can have me any way you want."

He couldn't think, much less respond. At her husky words, every bit of blood drained out of his brain. He had been propositioned plenty of times, but somehow when Jessica did it…

He looked down at her. She smiled, her eyes dark with arousal and promise. His hands tightened around her upper arms as he focused helplessly on her lips.

Jessica swayed toward him.

"Not here." Then he was cutting through the crowd, practically dragging her along with him.

In the elevator, he fumbled for the room key that would allow them access to the suites on the top floors. His hands felt big and awkward as they swiped the key through the reader. *If you stripped me naked on the hors d'oeuvres table…* Christ. She always had a way of knocking him off balance, of peeling away every last bit of self control. She had thrown the words out so casually, and as soon as she said them he had pictured doing just that—imagined shoving aside the crudités and shrimp cocktail and spreading her out like his own personal feast.

The doors closed and she was in his arms. He pushed her against the elevator wall, his tongue thrusting urgently into her mouth. She wound around him, humming incoherent words of encouragement. They weren't nearly close enough. She tilted her head back, inviting his tongue deeper. He was drowning in the taste of her when he felt her hands slide down between them. His body jerked.

They were still in the elevator. He was damned if he was going to make love in a public elevator. He managed to wrest her hands away from him and anchored them above her head with one of his own.

"*Not here.*" Could she hear the desperation in his voice?

She tilted her head back against the wall. With her arms up over her head, the motion thrust her breasts out. It was impossible not to look down; easier to stop breathing than to keep his eyes above her neck.

Her nipples were clearly visible under the thin silk halter top of her dress. He watched his own hands pushing aside the fabric, heard his own labored breathing as his thumb brushed across the tight peak. He wasn't aware of lowering his head until the sweet taste exploded on his tongue and he heard her moan.

The swish of the elevator doors slapped him back to sanity. He jerked the scrap of material back over her breast and sucked in some deep breaths. Was there a flash of triumph in her eyes? *Jesus.*

The bland normality of the hallway cleared his head. What the hell was he doing? They had barely said two words to each other.

Nothing about this night was going according to plan. He had to establish some rules. He had to let her know who was in charge or he was lost.

He looked down at her. What was she thinking? Was it so easy for her? Was it a game, a diversion? He held the door open. Waited. She hesitated, then flashed him a confident smile as she stepped past him.

Inside, he shrugged out of his jacket. "Second thoughts, Jessica?"

Brave words. He wasn't sure if he could really let her go at this point.

She shook her head and raised her chin a little until she looked him right in the eye.

No second chances.

He put his hand behind her head and pulled her to him. She tasted wild, and sweet, and he couldn't get enough of her. Just like that, just with a kiss, he felt himself going under.

He pulled back a little. See? In control.

"What was it you wanted in the elevator, Jessie?" He let his thumb brush across the silk covering one nipple. "Was it this?"

She clutched at his shirt, stared up at him with dazed eyes.

"No?" He rained kisses along her jaw to her ear. "This, then?" He began a slow circle around the nipple with his thumb.

She twisted against him, standing on tiptoe and tugging at his hair to pull his head down.

She was so beautiful. It hurt to look at her. He laughed softly to keep from moaning.

He leaned closer, so his lips just brushed her ear as he whispered, "Tell me, Jessie."

"Your mouth," she gasped.

It took everything he had to step away from her as she swayed toward him. "Well, then, let's see what you're offering. Take off your dress."

He should have known better. She brushed aside his attempt at intimidation. With a defiant glance, she unfastened the clasp at the back of her neck and let the dress slither to the floor. When her hand went to her Carnival mask he shook his head.

"Leave it." The words came out like gravel through his throat.

She inclined her head in acknowledgement, then raised her arms and turned in a graceful pirouette.

He forced air into his lungs. He was way out of his league. Stupid to think he could get the upper hand with her. He had expected a thong under the dress, but his imagination had obviously been too conservative. She was wearing what appeared to be a handful of ribbons that attached to a minuscule triangle of material in the front. The ribbons radiated out over her perfect ass into a tiny bow, then drew his eyes to where they disappeared below. In front of him, she pivoted proudly like a pagan goddess in her high heels, ribbons, and the jeweled mask.

*

Jessica stood her ground. She had been in front of cameras all her life. She knew that she was beautiful; that she could make him want her. Morgan's hot gaze and flushed face told her she wasn't wrong. At least she still had that small bit of power. It wasn't enough. It wasn't nearly enough, but for tonight it would do. She took a single step toward him and drew his head down to her.

When her knees buckled, she felt his arm circle her waist and he lowered her to the floor. His tongue circled and flicked at her nipple, while his hand reached down to cup her. He tugged at the damp ribbons of her thong, creating an unbearable pressure against her swollen flesh.

She lifted herself against his tormenting hand, trying to ease the ache he was creating. Immediately, he removed both his hand and his mouth.

"Shhh, not yet," he murmured.

She shifted toward him, reaching for his zipper. As in the elevator, he captured her hands and pulled them above her head.

"Uh, uh. Naughty Jessica, not until *I* say."

After that, the torture began. Morgan's hands and mouth were busy, first on her breasts, then lower, pushing her legs wide and stroking her to a fever pitch. He scraped the ribbons of her thong against her most sensitive skin, pushed them aside to plunge his tongue or his fingers into her depths. Each time, just when the bright promise of her orgasm was upon her, he pulled away. Again and again he moved up her body to torment her breasts or kiss her deeply.

"You taste so good, Jessie," he said in his dark voice. "I'm drunk on you. Taste yourself and see how good it is."

Finally, she was sobbing in frustration, trembling with desire. Despite his erotic words and the evidence of his erection, he was still fully clothed and in control.

"Please," she whispered.

He stilled next to her.

"Please, what, Jessie?"

"Please, come inside of me," she moaned.

He shifted next to her, reaching down to unzip and free himself. Then he was looking down and she was trapped in his gaze. He was poised just at her entrance. She strained her hips toward him, trying to impale herself on him.

"Say my name, Jessie," he said. "Say my name and tell me what you want."

"I want you, Morgan. Please," she begged. "Please, Morgan, I need you inside of me."

He gave a harsh groan and plunged into her. It was all she needed. She fell into the darkness and the fairy lights exploded around her.

*

Jessica came back to herself as Morgan picked her up off the floor and carried her into the next room. He deposited her on the bed, then pulled off his tie and began unbuttoning his shirt.

She struggled for some composure.

"That was nice," she said. "It must be late, though, I'd better get back downstairs."

Morgan tossed his shirt aside and began pulling off his pants. Her gaze locked on him in shock. He was still fully aroused.

"Nice?" He lifted one eyebrow as he shed the rest of his clothes. "Oh, no, Jessie," he said. "You promised I could have you any way I wanted. I've just gotten started."

*

Hours later, Jessica slid cautiously out of the big bed. Her body was sore, but sated in ways she couldn't have anticipated at the beginning of the night. Quietly, she padded back into the sitting room and slipped into the silk dress. Giving in to impulse, she tiptoed back to the bedroom door for a final look at her dark lover.

Moonlight from the open curtains washed the color from the room. In a tangle of sheets, Morgan's big body was the only solid thing in a ghostly landscape. Jessica knew lots of handsome men, but somehow none of them ever seemed quite as *real* as Morgan.

What would he do if she curled herself against his solid warmth and begged him to let her stay as she had begged him to take her?

She straightened and turned back toward the door. She was sex and scandal. She might be fun for a night, but he would not want her in the morning. She would spare them both that. Carrying her shoes, she let herself out of the suite.

*

In the bedroom, Morgan listened to the quiet snick of the door. Her exotic scent lingered in the room. It was a taunting reminder that he was there and she was gone. He could command her body for a night, but she would slip through his fingers in the light of day. Rolling onto his back, he stared sightlessly at the ceiling as his beautiful wife fled back to her glittering life.

Find our more about *Infamous* when you visit *www.crimsonromance.com/crimson-romance-ebooks/ crimson-romance-book-genres/spicy-romance-novels/infamous/*.

Also Available

In the mood for more Crimson Romance?
Check out *The Wicked Bad* by Karyn Gerrard
at CrimsonRomance.com.

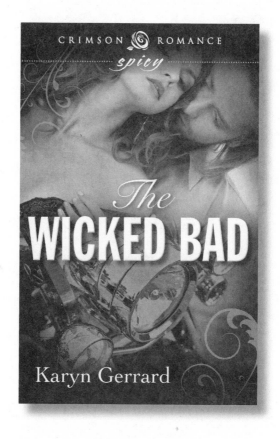